SECRET VENGEANCE

THE DONAVAN ADVENTURE SERIES
(VOLUME 6)

TOM HAASE

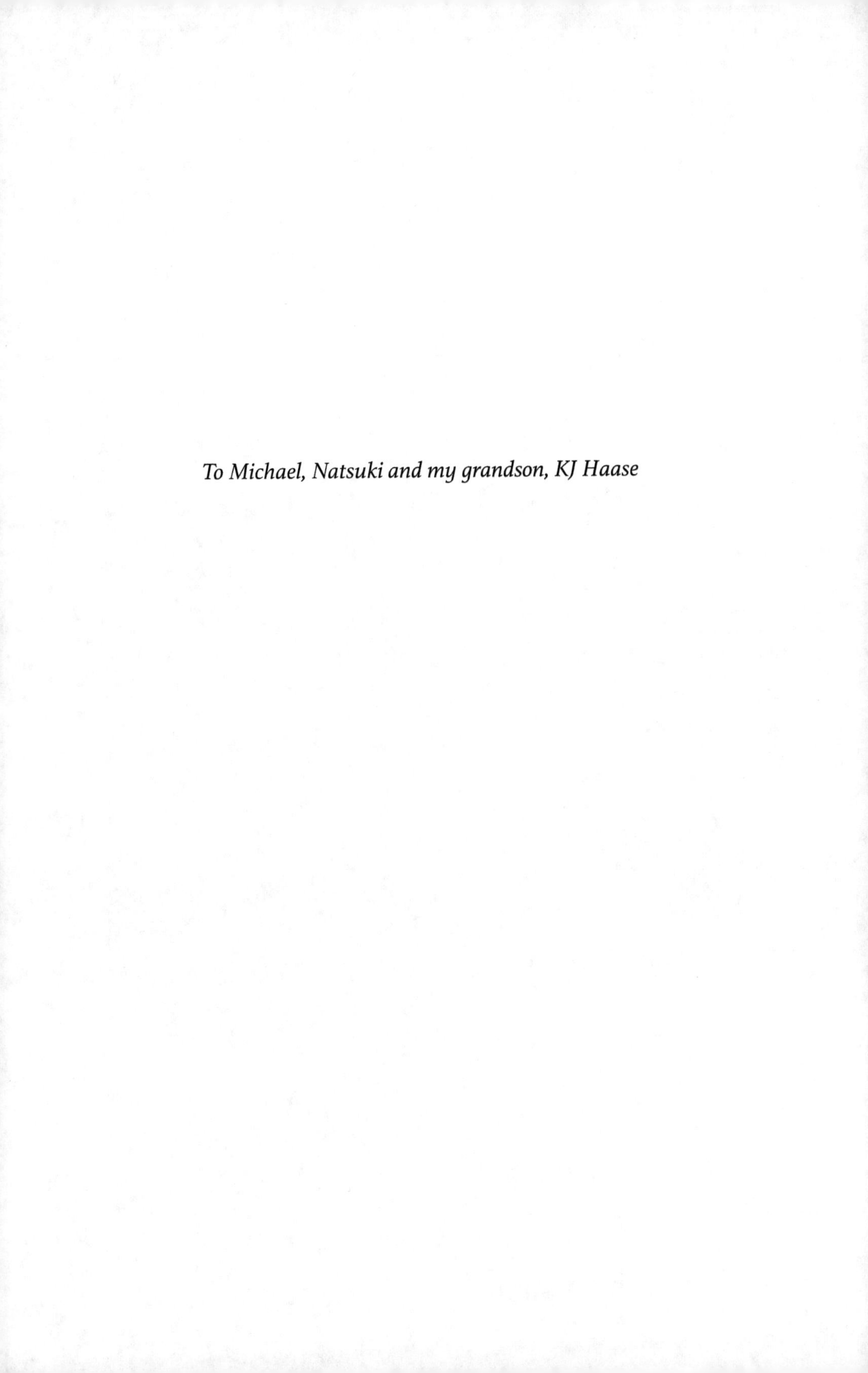

To Michael, Natsuki and my grandson, KJ Haase

ALSO BY TOM HAASE

THE DONAVAN ADVENTURE SERIES

Secret of the Oil

Secret Device

Secret of the Thorns

Secret of the Bibles

Secret of the Icon

Secret Vengeance

THE COASTAL ADVENTURE SERIES

Betrayed Angel

Betrayed Devil

Betrayed Friend (Winter 2018)

For the latest information on Tom's upcoming books, sign up for his free author newsletter at tomhaase.com/news.

FREE NOVELLA

To receive your free copy of the exclusive Donavan Adventure series novella *Secret of the Assassin* (not available anywhere else), visit **tomhaase.com/assassin.**

1

MYSTERY PHONE CALL

HE FLIPPED ON THE LAMP NEXT TO THE BED, PUNCHED TALK, AND jammed the receiver to his ear. Never one to sleep soundly, the man had opened his eyes at the first shrill sound of the cell phone. Four a.m. shined from the clock on the nightstand, like a beacon in the pitch dark of his bedroom. He'd like to kill the person who dared to wake him this early. He lifted his head off the pillow and quickly glanced at the face of the phone's digital display, which only blinked "Blocked Number" at him.

He waited. Whoever called needed to identify themselves before he would speak. This number was currently available only to a handful of people, but the call could come from anywhere in the world in his business, especially the Iranians, who didn't seem to care about the hour when they dialed his number.

After sucking in a deep breath, the man forced a long exhalation. He waited a few seconds more and then concluded that somebody had misdialed. He reminded himself to turn his phone off before going to bed. The man stretched out his arm to punch End, but then he heard a muffled cough emanate from the instrument.

"You were recommended to me, and I require your services," the voice declared, sounding like a computer-generated one, akin to the

Robocop vocal manipulation he'd heard recently in a movie. This intriguing touch captured his attention.

"I hope it's important. Is it?" the man demanded.

"I will make it worth your while," the disguised voice informed him.

"What do you need?" the man said.

"I have a contract for you," the altered voice intoned.

"I don't do contracts." The man shifted the phone to his other ear, expecting the voice to continue despite his denial.

"Don't insult me. I know who you are and what you can do. Now, let's talk money. I need a problem eliminated, and the fee I'm willing to pay is five million." Suddenly, the call commanded heightened interest. This presented an unexpected opportunity for immense profit. The man considered for a few seconds before he answered.

"I don't do anything for less than ten," he replied and waited.

The caller took his own time before he responded.

"Five now and five on completion," came from the disguised voice.

"What is this contract?" the man inquired.

"Believe me, this is one you will want to take. The details will arrive in your personal email in a moment. I expect it to be executed within the next few days. Time is of the essence. Agreed?"

"Wait a minute."

The man jumped out of bed and hit the wakeup bar on his desktop computer located on the far side of his bedroom. The machine's display lit up, illuminating the picture of his daughter sitting on the desktop, and a message popped up on the screen. He opened it, read it, looked at the attached pictures, and concentrated on the request for the bank information needed for the initial deposit of money. He viewed the sender's email address, undoubtedly one that would be deactivated very soon, and provided his account number in a one-line response.

"Agreed," the man said.

The line went dead.

He printed the message and returned to his bed, where he reread the words to ensure there was no mistake. There wasn't. His heart pounded in anticipation of getting the money. The contract would be easy to fulfill.

Eliminate Bridget and Scott Donavan as well as Matt Higgins. No collateral damage to anyone else.

2

ALEXANDRIA, VIRGINIA

9:40 P.M.

Bridget Donavan sat in the farthest corner of the U-shaped main bar. She faced the dance area, so it gave her a view of all approaches to her location. She twirled a swizzle stick in her martini after eating the last of three olives. Having consumed her second drink, she felt the effects of the alcohol begin to take hold as it became harder to focus her thoughts. She flipped a strand of her red hair out of her face before she took another sip.

This night, she had come to this semi-private club. The music played at a loud volume, which along with the chatter emanating from the bar flies, distorted the sound so it defied recognition as belonging to any particular musical genre. She couldn't actually understand any of the words being sung by a woman on the band-stand because of the noise level emanating from multiple gigantic speakers hanging from the ceiling. This didn't discourage dancing in the sardine-packed small floor, surrounded by tables occupied by customers in various stages of inebriation.

She hadn't heard from Matt for three days—not since they'd made love in Savannah on their last night there. She'd initially hoped their surrender to the palpable chemistry between them would be the beginning of a great future, both in their new business venture and in a renewed love life. She'd felt, for the first time in ages, the peace of a deep emotional connection to someone. An image of Matt popped into her mind. She'd watched him in the bathroom of their hotel room afterwards, with his dark sun-tanned face and his thick black hair. He often ran his fingers through it. He stood a little over six feet tall, the perfect height for her to nestle into his caress, and to place her lips on his.

As the days had passed with no contact from Matt, her initial hopes and dreams had begun to fade. Now, she rested on a stool, alone in a bar, waiting for a call that so far hadn't materialized. Twisting a dangling strand of hair, she fought against the depression that threatened to engulf her. That was why she'd escaped from the apartment tonight—she needed to get out and be with people.

The sex hadn't been a simple release of tension for them, she though. They'd killed a Russian arms dealer and taken down a home-grown terrorist cell, but she'd believed their lovemaking had been so much more than a simple pressure relief following the shoot-out and the crazy chase through the center of downtown Savannah, Georgia.

Did he think they were sex buddies now? She didn't believe that deep in her heart.

She'd decided for some stubborn reason to refuse to be the one to call first. In her mind, he must make the first move. She remembered how she'd almost involuntarily initiated that event in Savannah, and now it was his turn to reciprocate.

Bridget ordered her third drink. In the deep regions of her subconscious, she conceded there had to be a pressing reason for his silence. He would have to work it out in his mind, whether they were or were not going forward as a team.

So tonight, she'd decided not to sit in her brother's apartment and wait for his answer. She'd been staying with her brother, Scott, and his fiancée, Gerti, while searching for her own place in the Washington area. She'd halted the search based on what now seemed a false hope of cohabitation with Matt. At present, Scott and Gerti were away in New York, visiting her father. Scott had called her earlier today and informed her that he and Gerti had gotten married in a small civil ceremony. They would have a formal wedding in a few months, and all would be invited.

This revelation had caught her by surprise, although it wasn't totally unexpected because she'd overheard some of their future plans when they talked in the apartment. Nevertheless, he should have invited her to the informal service. She'd told him that. After all, she was his sister. She had shown her agitation to say the least, but knew deep in her heart that she would forgive him. Little brother had grown up, and he'd made his own way. She needed to concede that and she actually delighted in the news, and looked forward to the promised formal repeat.

"Excuse me," said a voice near her.

She turned from the bar, where she had been staring at her new drink, and surveyed the man standing behind her. A tall, striking, dark-skinned muscular man in an open white collared shirt, a blue blazer and khaki pants, smiled down at her.

"May I sit?" he queried.

She didn't nod, but only took a large sip from her glass. What stupidity. Thinking of a future with Matt, and now a stranger sat down next to her. She knew she should get up and leave.

"Care for a drink?" the man asked.

"Sorry, I'm just leaving." She decided to move away before she might change her mind.

"Such a shame—not even one dance?"

She stood up and instantly felt the effects of the drinks. She tried to make the bar stand still. After a few attempts, it settled down and she felt she could now walk. *Gotta leave by myself before I'm tempted to take this hunk of man home. That's the booze talking*, she thought. She understood the feeling and needed to exit immediately.

The man reached to steady her after she took two steps and swayed a little, trying to maintain her balance. He stood about the same height as she at five feet eleven.

"Come, let me escort you. My name is Daniel," he said. "What's yours?"

"Bridget," she responded and tried to head for the main door. She realized she had to get rid of this guy. She'd made up her mind and felt sure Matt would reach the correct conclusion in due time. They needed one another, now and in the future.

Get away from this Daniel.

Daniel maneuvered her toward a side exit rather than the front door, which remained blockaded with bodies dancing and drinking. "I think we can go out this way. Easier than trying the main entrance," he shouted next to her ear to allow her to hear him over the cacophony of noise surrounding them. Upon reaching the exit, he pushed the side door open and led her outside into an alley.

"This'll be a good place for us," she heard Daniel murmur.

Bridget knew she'd made a mistake in allowing this man to get so close to her in her present state. She didn't want sex from anyone but Matt, and now this stranger seemed to think she wanted some kind of quickie against the wall of an alley.

Her brain remained a little foggy, but Bridget decided to go back inside to lose this stranger. She loved Matt, she realized. And even if he didn't love her—and she didn't believe that—she couldn't experience meaningless sex with this Daniel guy.

The alley loomed dark around her. The night air hit her nostrils as the door slammed shut behind her, closing out the sounds of the club, leaving silence—a deadly silence. At that moment, Bridget's sense of danger triggered. She'd felt this intuition of imminent danger before—the subconscious awareness she'd gained on the battlefield—and she knew she must pay immediate attention to it. Not doing so had occasionally caused her pain in the past, but acting as soon as she felt the warning had saved her life on several occasions. Her combat training, on top of a tour in the Middle East, had permanently inculcated a sixth sense in her. That feeling buzzed on high alert in her head.

She straightened up and took a deep breath, deciding she would tell him she wanted to go inside for something she forgot. Hell no, this seemed a stupid move to delay. She would go home and call Matt. This waiting demanded an end, and it must culminate tonight. The time to make her move had arrived. She decided to act.

She pivoted away from the door to go down the alley. There she could reach the street and go home. She rotated back, and faced him to tell him she wanted to be alone, and to get away from her. As she turned, she saw the knife. God, she hated knives. In the microsecond it took for her mind to register the danger, Daniel plunged the weapon toward her heart.

She instinctively twisted with a rapid movement, but now the effects of all the alcohol slowed her reaction. The knife slashed across her neck and up the side of her face. The pain lit up the universe in front of her eyes. Then he plunged the blade into her chest. During the brief moment it had taken her to realize the danger she was in, the sharp end of the blade impaled her. With concentrated effort, she willed her defensive combat training to kick in. She rotated away and the knife pulled out.

Continuing her swivel, she reached out to grab the extended arm of her assailant. She used all the weight of her body to press down as she grabbed his wrist and twisted, while falling forward onto his outstretched appendage. She saw her own blood on the knife's blade. She felt the intense pain in her rib cage and the sting of the slice across her neck. The wet redness oozed out of her chest. She could smell the hot metallic odor of her own blood.

The attacker screamed as she allowed her weight to collapse onto his arm. She heard it snap, and her body maneuvered to be on top of his outstretched hand when he landed. She knew she must act fast as her life force would leave her soon. Her efforts resulted in the man releasing his weapon.

Bridget caught the knife in midair with her right hand. Daniel continued his fall toward the alley pavement, while she maintained her downward pressure. She pressed her weight onto his arm. In a last effort, she used the remainder of her strength to propel her right arm upward. With a mighty energy erupting from her final desperation, she plunged the point of the blade up into her attacker's throat right under his chin, forcing it up into his brain. The resulting blood spray covered her face.

Exhausted, she collapsed to the asphalt, landing on top of her dead attacker. No one else appeared from the exit door. She thought it might need to be opened from the inside. Her energy now ebbed as she mustered the last of it to reach into her pocket as she rolled off the man. She withdrew her cell, and when the screen lit up, she saw the time: 9:45 p.m. She hit the speed dial number for Matt, located in her favorites. It rang, and finally his voice. She heard him say something, and then in a few seconds he called her name, but a gurgling sound was the only thing she could produce as blood came from her mouth.

"Matt, I love you," were the words she unsuccessfully attempted to say as darkness enveloped her.

3

—————

NEW YORK, NY

8:55 P.M.

Scott Donavan rose to his feet as he watched Gerti pivot between tables and people to reach his table. The two of them would, at last, have a chance to celebrate without her father being present. Scott and Gerti had arrived at her home in New York from Savannah. After his recovery in the hospital, they'd announced to her father their intention to marry. On Gerti's insistence, her father had arranged a private civil ceremony.

Scott had called Bridget to tell her after the fact. A formal wedding, he told her, was planned for some time in the near future, to which all family members would be invited. Bridget had sounded a little miffed, but she'd forgive him. She always did, whenever he did something to upset her.

They'd been married in the morning at the city clerk's office with Gerti's father as a witness. After they'd been pronounced husband and wife, Benjamin Schultz had welcomed Scott into the family with a handshake, but no pat on the back.

Now Gerti had entered the wine bar a half hour after Scott—later than he'd expected, because of their earlier-agreed-on time. She hadn't answered her cell despite his repeated attempts to contact her, so all he could do was wait.

She reached his side and let out a whoosh of breath as she placed a hand on his and rose on tiptoes. He leaned over his drink to give her a kiss. She walked around the table and sat, and he poured her a glass of champagne.

"Do you realize what's happened in our lives since we met?" he said. "It's absolutely unbelievable. I'm the luckiest guy in the world, and I love you so much."

"Besides the numerous adventures we've shared, this new one will be a lifetime commitment," Gerti said. "I've come to love you, more than I thought I could ever love anyone." She gave him a radiant smile that lit up her eyes. "Sorry I'm late, but I had to make quick stop."

Scott stole a glance around. He noticed two Muslim women with their heads covered, casting sideways glances in their direction. For a non-drinking group of people, they seemed out of place here. This watering hole contained so many patrons that it was standing room only around the bar. Before the late rush-hour drinkers arrived, he had secured a two-person table.

She tugged him closer and kissed him deep, giving him a taste of her tongue.

"What's that for?" he asked.

"For marrying me, for starters, but also for something else. I remind you that we've only been married for one day. But I have news that most couples must wait months to receive."

"Would you like to drink some of your champagne? I got it to celebrate."

She didn't answer, but waved the waiter over. "A glass of Perrier, please."

"What's that about?" he queried.

He poured himself a drink from the bottle of Dom Pérignon for this special occasion to toast their nuptial. They'd previously agreed that tonight they would discuss where they would take their honeymoon, and also where to live in the near future. She knew that he didn't want to stay in her apartment, where her father resided, but somehow he suspected she would push for that, at least for a short time. Maybe she'd reached some form of arrangement with her father for his quick approval of their marriage, and that's what she wanted to convey.

He looked at her and thanked his stars for his extreme good luck. Although their initial contact in the Smithsonian had proven disastrous, and a little humorous, he'd found his soul mate and his best friend in the same person. The gunshot wound he'd received in Savannah continued to heal, but he didn't want her to use that as a reason to move in with her father. The point where the bullet entered still hurt, but not that much.

He took in her beauty, as he adored her close-cropped jet-black hair, the light olive-toned skin, and her fine sculpted body. Her blue eyes—in reality, stunning sky-blue eyes—were offset by the soft red lipstick. The silver medal hanging around her neck contrasted with the lovely skin tone she inherited from her deceased mother.

"Sit back and relax. I have something to say. I don't know how you'll take it, but it's important." She took a sip of her water. "We've known one another for a long time, as modern relationships go, and we've been lovers for months. Are you ready for this, newly married man that you are?" she asked.

"For what? What did you do, love?" He gave her a wide grin.

"We did." She gleamed as she revealed this. "You're going to be a father."

Scott choked on the champagne he'd just sipped, and almost spat it directly at Gerti. His mind raced. A father. Not possible. *Oh, my god!*

A slow smile spread across his face until it encompassed his eyes as they conveyed his inner happiness. He grabbed her hands. "Really?" he managed to get out.

"Yes, really," she affirmed.

"I'm going to be a father?"

She nodded.

He stood up and leaned in to give her a hug. He backed off when he started to squeeze her.

"Don't be silly. I'm not fragile now. But no more drinks for me. That's why the water."

"I wanted to order another bottle, but I won't," he said.

"Good. You finish this one and then we'll go tell my father."

"Let's go now," Scott urged.

"Not yet. I came in his limo, so we can use it. His bodyguards came with me. They parked the car outside. I requested they stay out there so we could enjoy a little privacy. So now, are you happy?"

"Ecstatic. How far along are you?"

"About ten weeks."

"Is it a boy or a girl?" Scott held her hands as he asked this question.

"How the hell should I know? The doctor only told me before I came here. I knew after missing my period, and taking the test, but I kept it from you till I had it confirmed by the doc. We'll find out together on a subsequent visit, when they do a sonogram."

Scott let his mind wander. He ran through some of the adventures they had experienced together. Their first meeting, when he'd bumped into her in the Smithsonian, could be classified as a total flop. Later, when her father had given him the money to pursue the Constantine Bible, they'd made a real connection. Then a few weeks after that, when his sister, Bridget, had rescued her father, was when things had progressed to more than a passing interest by both.

In Savannah, Gerti had saved his life after he had taken a bullet meant for her, and she'd rushed him to an emergency room using every asset at her command. In the hospital, they'd used the time to tell one another their true feelings. He loved her and wanted to be married. She said she wanted the same thing. So now, they were, and in the next breath it seemed he would be a father.

"I'm so happy," he said.

"Do you think we should tell Father now or wait till we find out if it is a boy or a girl?" Gerti asked.

"We'll have to sooner or later. He isn't blind." Scott poured himself another glass.

"Remember, no more alcohol for me," Gerti said. She reached over and squeezed Scott's hand. "Let's go tell him. I'll call the limo and tell them we're ready." She called, and after Scott finished his glass of champagne, they moved toward the front door.

They exited the wine bar, and Scott saw the long black car parked some distance away at the curb with two men standing outside. He escorted Gerti toward the car. The security men started to open the doors.

"Wait," Gerti blurted out. "I left my purse at the table. I'll go get it."

"Let me," Scott said.

"No, wait here." She turned and headed back into the bar.

Scott went over to the limo. The man at the passenger side waved at Scott, and the driver came around to the sidewalk without starting the car to meet him. "Hi, there."

"Where have you guys been?"

"We parked and had some eats. How's it going with you?" the man asked.

"Super. We need to go to see Mr. Schultz. We have some great news for him," Scott said.

"What's the news?" the driver asked as he came to face Scott.

"That'll have to wait till we tell him," Scott said.

The two security guards nodded in unison.

Scott looked back and saw Gerti emerging from the wine bar, still a good hundred feet away. He hurried toward her and put his hands on her shoulders to stop her. He hugged her. "I really am so happy."

He started to move them toward the limo. The driver got into the car. A moment later, Scott heard a click instead of the roar of an engine. Too slow, his mind registered the danger, but he rotated to protect Gerti from what he expected to happen. The explosion propelled Scott against Gerti, who smacked against the wall behind her after Scott's body slammed into her from the outward pressure of the blast. They both ricocheted off the building's brick side.

Scott landed on top of her. He rolled off as fast as he could manage and staggered to his feet. He saw a burning hulk of metal, all that remained of the car. Although his head pounded, he turned and looked back at Gerti. He observed a large amount of blood on the sidewalk beneath her head.

His head hurt like hell. He tried to think—what to do, how to help Gerti. She opened her eyes. He recognized her sluggish eye movement as a potential indication of real danger. He needed to concentrate, to act. He picked her up and scanned the area, searching for assistance. He didn't see the bodyguard, who had stood outside the vehicle, but assumed the man to be injured. His focus turned back to Gerti, whose eyes were now closed. A short distance away, he saw a taxi come to a stop at the curb. He rushed to it and opened the door. He placed Gerti on the backseat and ordered the driver to take them to the nearest hospital.

He looked at his watch.

It displayed 9:45 p.m.

4

ALEXANDRIA, VIRGINIA

9:40 P.M.

MATT HIGGINS JOGGED ALONG THE PATH THAT FOLLOWED THE GEORGE Washington Parkway, winding along beside the Potomac River from the District of Columbia to Mount Vernon, the home of the first president. He jogged within half a mile of his apartment in the Old Town area of Alexandria. Rain had started to fall twenty minutes earlier, sending the majority of evening joggers home. He now enjoyed the trail almost all to himself.

The mind games he'd played with himself over the last three days after their arrival from Savannah still plagued him. The quandary he wrestled with wasn't what to do, but how to do it. It took two days for it to crystallize in his brain. Never had he taken that much time to decide on anything. This decision would change the course of his life.

The problem, and the solution, focused on one person, Bridget Donavan. He knew he loved her more than life. After deep contemplation, he'd decided to ask her to marry him if she would. He'd even gone to a local jeweler where he'd bought an engagement ring this afternoon. His whole life now revolved around Bridget. He would call her after he reached home and got cleaned up. He needed to see her tonight. He couldn't wait any longer to propose. He would explain to her why it had taken him so long to reach the conclusion that he knew already existed deep in his heart.

The rain continued to come down and seemed to be gaining in intensity. He noticed a priest sauntering by under an umbrella, presumably out for an evening stroll. Funny time to do it in this weather, he mused, but he decided not to pay any attention to the thought. He ran on and increased his stride to get home quicker, now that he'd reached his final decision. He'd been stupid for not contacting her already. After the night they'd spent together in Savannah, he subconsciously knew then what he needed to do—no, what he wanted to do.

The two of them had performed admirably as a team in Savannah. He knew they could continue to do that, even if they were married. No problems were too difficult to surmount. His job at the S.O.E. (Special Operations Executive) would provide a framework for their new company, and the director had previously congratulated him on capturing the arms dealer cum terrorist named Karim. That operation had destroyed the largest weapons-importing business, run by a Russian warlord's nephew. The organization had catered primarily to terrorists on the East Coast, and they had taken it down.

He remembered how Bridget had pursued the dealer down the steep steps of Savannah's historic district, even as the man fired at her. The man, Michael Alexander Alexandrovitch, had shot her brother, whom she thought dead. She'd cornered him, but there wasn't any dialogue—no questions, no chitchat like in the movies. She had taken aim, fired point-plank, and walked away without ever looking back.

As his mind digested these thoughts, he hadn't given any attention to the jogger approaching from his rear. The man stepped in a puddle on the asphalt, and that splashing noise brought Matt back to his wet surroundings. He rotated his head toward the sound and saw a man wearing a dark tracksuit coming fast, intending to pass him. He moved over to allow passage, then turned back around to watch where he stepped while he continued his jog.

In his peripheral vision, he caught sight of the jogger as the man started to pass him. The man reached into his pocket, which caused Matt to focus on him. There would be no reason to do that, running as fast as this man was. When the hand reappeared with a rapid movement, the jogger held out a gun. He aimed the weapon at Matt's head as the assailant moved directly beside him. This all happened in the time it took for him to take two strides in his jog.

Matt ascertained the imminent danger, and his lightning reflexes kicked in. He rotated toward the man, not away from him, collapsing partially to the ground to get below the level of the weapon, and swung his legs out in front of the man. This encounter had quickly become a life-and-death combat fight. No time to draw his own piece. Matt felt his right shin make contact with the leg of the running assailant.

The force exerted by Matt's leg did the trick. The attacker yelled as he tripped. The man began to tumble forward but managed to fire three rounds in Matt's direction. All missed, but a shard from the asphalt grazed Matt's ear as he rolled away and simultaneously pulled his Glock from his belt. The rain fell into his eyes in his supine position, but he focused on the front sight of his weapon. When it landed on the attacker's center of mass, he fired two bullets into the man's chest. Both of Matt's rounds entered the target. The assailant's gun slid from his hand.

Matt's heart pounded so loud in his ears that he thought he might lose his balance as he attempted to get up. It took him a few seconds to hear the phone ringing in his pocket. The noise barely overshadowed the thumping in his chest. With some effort he extracted the cell and saw 9:45 p.m. Bridget's telephone number displayed on the phone's screen.

Now his heart stopped a second. He wasn't ready to speak with her, but he might as well do it now rather than a half hour from now. He hit talk on the display and placed the phone near his ear.

"Hi, you won't believe what just happened," he said. He waited on a response. As none came, he assumed she wanted him to say more. "I've been meaning to call you. We have some important things to discuss."

He listened. Nothing. "Bridget" he said. His heart still pounded in his ears, but that intensified on not hearing her voice.

"Bridget," he shouted into the phone. What the hell was she trying to do?

He went quiet. He barely heard the gurgling noise of someone struggling to talk after being wounded. He remembered this sound from before, when he had encountered it in the desert, after a soldier had taken a bad hit. Why did he hear it now? Nothing now came from his speaker.

He went to the app on his phone to find friends. After a few seconds, Bridget's location was displayed—an alley off King Street, less than half a mile away. He knew something had gone drastically wrong. He searched his attacker for ID and found none. His mind registered that the man must be a pro, and someone must have hired him to carry out this attack. Why didn't that surprise him? Then he checked the man's pulse. None. He started running toward Bridget's location.

Matt speed-dialed Liz Garcia at the FBI, who acted as his handler/helper on behalf of the director. He and Bridget did off-book operations for the director, and he needed Liz to take care of the downed man. A month ago, the director of the FBI had recruited him to set up a black ops section, answering solely to him through Liz as his contact. After telling her what happened, and that he thought Bridget must be in some trouble, Matt gave her Bridget's location.

"I'm only a few blocks away. I'll meet you there," Liz said as he disconnected.

He ran toward Bridget's phone and increased his speed to his maximum pace.

His phone buzzed in his hand. It was Scott, Bridget's brother. No time for him now; he was in New York. He held the display up in front of him and followed the map to Bridget's position.

He rounded the corner into the alley and momentarily froze. His heart jumped into his mouth at the horrific scene before him.

$$5$$

NEW YORK, NY

9:40 P.M.

Scott cradled Gerti's head, pressing his handkerchief against the blood gushing from the head wound. The material soaked through in a matter of seconds. He maneuvered around to remove his shirt and used it to replace the soaked and useless handkerchief.

"Can't you drive any faster?" he shouted at the taxi driver.

"I'm trying, buddy. Another two, maybe three minutes," the man said, with what Scott took to be a heavy Indian or Pakistani accent.

The driver honked his horn to encourage traffic to move out of his path, but Scott couldn't observe any immediate results. He willed the cab to get her to the emergency room faster. From where he sat, he couldn't do anything more for Gerti. His mind spun around as he closed his eyes forcing away thoughts of the dreadful scene in front of the wine bar.

While he kept pressure on the wound, he reached into his pocket to retrieve his cell. Taking a quick look down at Gerti, he saw his efforts seemed to be stemming the blood flow. His sister's number appeared on his speed dial menu, and he touched it. Her phone went to voice mail after four rings. Then he dialed Matt, in case they were together. He didn't know what either one of them could do for him at this time, but his mind told him to do it. Matt's cell produced the same negative result.

He knew the next call he would make needed to be to her father. On second thought, he tried Matt again but achieved the same outcome. Somehow, he knew from his short history with his new father-in-law that Mr. Schultz would go nuts over this. Scott's phone rang and on the screen he saw Schultz's number. His security people had probably already informed the men about the explosion, and his rushing Gerti off in a taxi. He decided to let it go to voicemail. He would call as soon as they got to the hospital. Then, after Gerti received medical attention, he would have something to tell her father.

The hospital's red emergency entrance sign appeared in the windshield. Relaxing a bit, Scott bent over and gave Gerti a gentle kiss on her forehead. "I love you," he whispered.

Ratcheting the door open even before the taxi stopped, he stepped out as soon as it did. He noticed an EMT crew walking to a parked ambulance outside the entrance to the emergency room.

"Help, I have a victim of a car bomb in here. Help me," he shouted.

The EMTs ran to the car and immediately took charge. One went to retrieve a rolling gurney, and the other started checking her vitals. In less than a minute, they took her into an examination room inside the hospital and treated her head wound as they waited for a doctor to examine her.

"You need to go to the lobby to go give your information at the front desk," the EMT said. He continued to carefully examine Gerti's head. "I'm not the doc, but I don't think she's that severely hurt. From the crack on the head she took, you can plan on her having one hell of a headache in the morning."

Scott breathed a sigh of relief. He went to the reception desk and filled out the required paperwork, then paid the waiting taxi driver. He could no longer put off the call. When Schultz answered, he dispensed with any greeting.

"She's fine," Scott said. "Or at least she will be. The doctor is with her now and is treating her head wound. They won't let me see her till they're finished."

"Are you injured?" Schultz asked.

"No, but what about your men?"

"One is dead. The other is now with the police. Did you see anyone or suspect anything?"

"Nothing. We were coming to see you for a surprise, but that can wait. I also can't reach my sister or Matt Higgins," Scott said.

"I'm in my car now. Where are you?" Schultz asked.

Scott told him. Based on the distance Schultz would have to travel, Scott estimated it would be a good twenty minutes before Schultz could arrive at the hospital. Surprisingly, Scott had become a little fond of the old man, and over the months, he felt a mutual bond of respect beginning to form. He hoped his father-in-law liked him, and he did seem pleased with their marriage. There remained, however, some lingering doubts in his mind. Many times in the past, he and his sister had held contrary views and taken actions contrary to those Mr. Schultz desired. His daughter had almost suffered death on the last venture he and Bridget had undertaken, and that hadn't sat well with her father. Scott believed the old man possessed a long memory.

"The stupid bastards who did this to my daughter will pay," Schultz said in a voice that conveyed pure hatred for the people responsible for his daughter's injury. Then he closed the connection.

Twirling his phone in his hand, Scott again tried to reach his sister. Someone answered it, but then the line went dead.

6

ALEXANDRIA, VIRGINIA

9:45 P.M.

MATT GASPED IN HORROR. HE COULD SEE BRIDGET'S BRIGHT RED HAIR illuminated by the streetlight in the alley. He wanted to ward off this ugly spectacle, make it go away, as if it never happened, but his eyes took in the scene. He ran toward the supine body of the woman he loved. Before reaching her, he noticed the large quantity of blood splattered on the asphalt. It trickled like a small river into the nearby drain.

"Bridget," he shouted. He knelt down beside her body, and with great care, he turned her face toward him. Her eyes were open, and to his horror, they appeared lifeless. He had previously witnessed that look in her eyes in the eyes of dead men in combat. He pressed his fingers to her throat. He hoped against hope, but couldn't detect one. Now tears began to flood down his face. He'd arrived too late. Never again would he hear her voice, her laugh, and never again feel her warm lips on his.

His mind called forth images of their turbulent relationship. He didn't want to do this, but looking into her beautiful face triggered the response, and he had no control over it. At that time, they'd served together in a special DIA unit to hunt down terrorists. They'd stopped a nuclear explosion from destroying the West's oil supply and saved a precious icon worth millions to Jews in Italy who were the victims of Nazi oppression. On their last mission, they'd killed a Russian arms dealer who pandered to homegrown terrorists in Savannah, and there they had shared their love.

His cell vibrated. He picked it out of his pocket because the real world still existed. He hit the answer button on the call from Scott, but decided to kill it. He needed a few more minutes with the woman he loved, before the realm of officialdom closed in and all this became a police scene.

In his mind, they were going to be married and get out of the FBI business. They embodied the skills and talents required to set up their own security and investigation company that didn't have to play the high-risk stakes of state terrorism and a government's nuclear games. On this last thought, he let his hand caress hers and he looked into her now-clouded eyes.

"Will you marry me, Bridget Donavan?" He could not control his grief. He let the tears gush down his cheeks. They came like a flooding river down his face and dripped onto hers.

"Matt, is she?"

He rotated his head toward the voice of Liz Garcia, who rushed up to where he knelt beside Bridget.

"I think so. I don't feel a pulse. Look at the blood. It appears that she killed her attacker." He wiped his tears away before he stood.

The door of the bar opened, and a man in an apron looked out, carrying a trash bag for depositing in the nearby dumpster.

"Dial 911 and get the police," Matt shouted at him. He realized he hadn't done that.

"I already did," Liz informed him.

The man looked around in a state of shock on seeing the murder scene. Then he nodded and disappeared back inside.

Matt forced himself to focus and to regain some control. He reached down and gently closed Bridget's eyes. She rested next to her assailant, who she had somehow been able to slay. The man bore a knife stuck in his neck, pointing up toward his brain. Death would have been almost instantaneous. Bridget knew how to kill.

He spoke in a subdued voice to his lover so that no one could hear. "I'm so sorry, my love. If I had given you the ring earlier, you wouldn't be here. I swear to you that whoever's behind this is a dead man walking." He felt the internal heat of rage building in his body. He would carry out his promise, and not stop till he succeeded.

Liz searched the attacker but found no ID or phone—another professional. The FBI might be able to identify him from fingerprints.

"Liz, I need your help." Matt now faced her.

"Wait. You have to get away from here. I'll handle this scene. You go and go now." After she'd found Bridget's location, she had called the city police, and they could be heard arriving with blaring sirens. "I'll have an FBI team here in a few minutes. Are you all right, Matt?"

"Hell no. I'm gonna get whoever ordered this. Liz, this appears to be a professional hit, and someone has to be behind it. They targeted me too. I have to contact Scott to warn him."

"Do it. But I can hear the anger in your voice. Stay calm. I know what she meant to you, but we'll find out what happened. Now, let me get on this. You get away from here this minute. We don't want you exposed as an FBI agent. I'll get back to you after I take care of this scene. Now please go." He could hear Liz suck in a great gulp of air, showing her exasperation about this situation. He recognized her ability to "take care of the scene," and he didn't need to stay here. Nothing remained for him to accomplish by staying around. If he did, he would be stuck for hours and not able to immediately start the search for the organizer of the attacks. He recognized them as being connected and orchestrated. His abilities were now needed in the fulfillment of the promise he'd made to bring down the culprit behind this murder, the dead man walking of his oath.

Every fiber in his body radiated anger. He felt the increase in the throbbing of his heart as he stared at the body of his beloved. He pounded his chest with his fists to release the building tension. It produced no relief.

"Liz, I can only promise you one thing—someone is going to die, after I make them suffer."

He hurried off seconds before the police appeared.

7

WASHINGTON, D.C

TWO DAYS LATER

MATT ARRIVED IN THE CEMETERY BEFORE THE HEARSE. THE BLACK SUIT and tie felt tight on his body, as the exterior trappings of mourning were all that held in the fury raging inside. He took another deep breath to try to remain outwardly calm.

The nondenominational service at the church lasted but twenty minutes. He now watched with a searing hatred in his gut as the military pallbearers placed the casket of a former soldier above the open grave. He used all his willpower to remain in control. This wouldn't be the time to break down. Matt sat in his chair, not hearing the words of the minister, but becoming more agitated by the minute. His mind raced over his life with Bridget. He remained in this state, until he stood when the others did, and then heard the volley of shots from the honor guard. The most difficult test of his strength was when the bugler played "Taps." He realized, as the last notes of the final tribute by the military faded, that the time for unabashed grief had passed. Now the need for action became paramount in his consciousness.

"It was a beautiful ceremony," Gerti said to Scott.

"I agree. The military know how to honor their own. We did the right thing by not having an open casket. I want to remember my sister the way I last saw her. Not sliced up and..." Scott faltered, but showed no sign of tears.

"Matt, are you all right?" Gerti asked. She had observed the wetness on his cheeks. He didn't respond, so she wondered if Matt concurred with Scott's decision on the casket, but decided not to ask.

Matt nodded. The depth of his grief now contained no tears, only a searing hatred, and a wave of burning vengeance ripping through his heart for whoever had orchestrated Bridget's murder. His primary mission in life became the elimination of the individual or individuals responsible, no matter how long it took, no matter what the cost. He would get it done.

Matt noticed that Schultz had increased his own personal protection after the recent events, and his expanded team accompanied him wherever he went. Matt assumed this enlarged guard detail also had protecting Gerti as one of its mission objectives.

The honor guard departed, and then the minister walked over to convey his condolences to Scott as the sole immediate relative in attendance. Scott quickly stood up to shake his hand, the bullet slammed into his vacated chair. He immediately crouched, falling sideways as he grabbed Gerti, and pulled her to the ground beside him, keeping her away from the spot of the first round's impact. The second hit right next to his head and missed his wife by mere inches. Someone among the mourners screamed.

Out of the corner of his eye, Matt saw Scott watching him as he ducked and dropped to the ground, while starting to survey the area. Scott appeared to have picked up on the fact that Matt's eyes now focused on the hill above the cemetery where he thought he saw movement. They both realized simultaneously the rounds came from that general elevated location. Matt rose, and grabbed Liz, his FBI liaison, pulling her away from the scene. Matt witnessed a pair from Schultz's extra security detail rush to the spot from which he thought the shots had originated.

Immediately after the crack of the shots had dissipated, Matt saw a man raise up and start to run away from the spot where he thought the shots originated. Matt felt his heart increase because of the pounding in his chest. People around him were shoving others to get out of the area. A woman screamed a piercing wail behind him. It caused him to wince, but he watched as two Schultz men rushed to the shooter's position. One of them jerked the shooter upright. The other held a gun on the man.

The FBI protection in the area consisted of only those around their director, who had attended out of respect for Matt. There existed no apparent threat to anyone else at the cemetery. Matt observed one of Schultz's security men slap the suspect with his hand and then pistol-whip him as they dragged their captive away band disappeared from sight in a few seconds. He didn't know if the FBI men had even seen this as they swarmed around the person of the director.

Chaos reigned around the casket. People were shouting and had stated to run to their cars. Matt saw Liz pull her phone out. He guessed that she had called to reinforce the original team who had accompanied the director to the funeral. Liz's action would bring the cavalry, if his bodyguards with him hadn't already made the same call. She headed toward the road to meet the FBI reinforcements on their arrival. During the same time, the director of the FBI signaled Matt to follow him, and then led him a distance away from the others.

* * *

SCHULTZ RUSHED TO WHERE GERTI NOW STOOD BESIDE SCOTT, HAVING regained her footing. He hugged his daughter and let out a loud curse at whoever had attempted to murder her. After he released her, Schultz called for his security team. Once order was reestablished in the area, Scott escorted Gerti back to a chair and guided her down. Schultz motioned Scott to accompany him, and they moved a short distance away, with Scott continuing to scan the horizon for any sign of a new threat.

"What do you have?" Scott asked.

"My men nabbed the shooter and are taking him to a secure

place. The FBI guys arrived too late, so they found nothing but the shell casings."

"I'll have to tell Matt. He'll want to interrogate him," Scott said.

"Not until my men get first crack at him. I want to find out why he shot at my daughter."

"What about me?"

"You too, of course," Schultz said, failing to look at Scott.

Scott nodded. He walked back to Gerti, and stayed there waiting until the cops came with the inevitable paperwork and questions. Police sirens wailed, signaling their approach, and the rotating multi-colored lights drew near.

* * *

MATT HUDDLED WITH THE DIRECTOR AS THEY MOVED AWAY FROM THE confusion around the burial plot. They were now far enough away from the others not to be heard, and he waited, anticipating his boss would speak first. After long seconds, Matt decided to break the silence.

"I know these events are a conspiracy to kill the four of us. It's obvious. Whoever's doing it is targeting Scott, Gerti and me now that they've eliminated Bridget. That's not going to happen. It's time for me to go on the offensive. I want you to assign me to this. I will wreak justice on the one who ordered Bridget killed. I want not only the killer, but whoever paid for these hits on Scott and Gerti too."

"Hold on, Matt." The director raised his hands. "I don't want you going off on a revenge crusade. We're still sworn officers in law enforcement."

"That I understand. I'll do this like any other mission we've conducted in the past. My intent is to capture them"—he smiled —"unless they shoot first."

"There has to be more to this than random individual attacks," said the director after a long pause. "You were all attacked at about the same time in different locations, from what we can put together. That smells like some organization targeting FBI assets. Your new mission is to find out why and to bring them to justice. Is that clear enough? Use Liz for your contact as before."

He shook Matt's hand, and they walked to his car. The police had arrived, and they recognized the director of the FBI. They didn't delay his departure from the cemetery.

As the director left, Matt remembered his clandestine meeting with the director that had set up his current position.

* * *

Hotel
Downtown D.C.

"As you know," the Director said, "most of the letter agencies —CIA, DIA, NSA, etc.—all possess what in the jargon is known as black ops capability. They are able to conduct operations completely off-book. The FBI has no such unit. I am proposing, with your help, that we create one."

Matt watched the director to see if he intended to laugh, and this meeting was merely a joke. His mind didn't comprehend in any detail the director's proposal.

"I'm sorry, sir. I think you're going to have to break this down, and explain in specific terms that I can get my head around. You've obviously thought it through, and I'm coming in on the end of that process."

"You're right, Matt, very perceptive and quite correct. Let me spell it out," the director said. "I want you to set up a team of people we can call upon to do jobs that would not be possible via the ordinary and regular channels of operation in the FBI. You will be a full-fledged agent, who reports only to me. Now, I'm not always available, and you worked quite well with an agent in that case of the terrorist on the Metro. I have assigned Special Agent Liz Garcia to be my special assistant. She will be your contact, and the person you will report to for whatever assets you need."

Matt knew Liz, a beautiful woman with alluring jet-black hair and perfectly shaped shoulders over an eye-candy body—and an attitude that could stop a charging bull.

The director interrupted his recollection. "You'll be given a specific mission given to you for each new operation. Don't use Bureau personnel for your ops."

Matt remained absolutely astounded at this proposal.

"As you can see, my mind's working overtime to comprehend the significance of what you're saying. I'm supposed to build a team, none of them from the FBI, and go after those who are providing arms to our homegrown terrorists or whatever other bad guys you designate. I'll have all the assets of the FBI available to me going through your office. Is that correct?"

"Exactly. I want to be very clear—I'm not giving you a 007 license to kill, but if for some reason you manage to get them to shoot at you first, I hope we're not going to experience any trials." The director took a big sip of his beer. "I want you to keep your connection with the FBI secret. Only you have the access. Don't show your badge unless absolutely necessary. This is an off-book operation. I'll make a note in your file about your new duties, but it will be in Garcia's hands to prevent anyone from personnel or any other snoop from finding it. Are you with me?"

"Yes, I think so."

Matt calculated some details—what kind of team he might put together, and the timeframe he would require. He needed to switch back into his military operational mode for the organization part, and rely on the vast FBI bureaucracy to supply him with the items he believed would be required. His detailed knowledge of all the assets in the Bureau would be invaluable in this operation. Yes, a great challenge loomed before him.

"Are you agreeable?" the director asked and waited for an answer.

"Yes."

"Welcome to the special operations executive that we just created," the director said.

"You mean like the old SOE from the Second World War? The precursor to the CIA?"

"Yes, sorta like that. I hadn't connected it, but a good catch on your part. We just produced a modern-day clandestine SOE operating within the FBI."

* * *

As the head of the FBI drove away from the cemetery, a commotion erupted behind Matt. He turned to see Scott supporting Gerti as she started to collapse. Her father rushed to her side.

Matt sprinted to where Scott held his wife.

"What's wrong?" he heard Schultz ask.

"She fainted. I have to get her to a hospital. It may be the pregnancy," Scott said.

"What pregnancy?" Schultz asked.

"Hers. You're going to be a grandfather. Now I need to rush her to a hospital for medical attention," Scott shouted at the man.

Schultz called someone on his phone, and within a minute, a car came screaming up to their position. A man got out and helped Scott put Gerti in the vehicle. Scott jumped in and they took off.

Schultz peered at Matt with a weird expression. Matt didn't remember ever seeing that look on the man's face before, and as soon as it appeared, it vanished. "Did you know about this pregnancy?"

"No. Not till now," Matt responded.

"Lucky I had another car ready as a backup. After the events in New York, I decided to double the security around Gerti and also myself. I'll call Scott so he can keep me informed of what's happening with Gerti. I'll be going there shortly. But first a visit to my men." His facial features completely changed before he said, "Imagine that, a grandfather."

It took another half hour to placate the local police, and then Matt drove out of the cemetery. Schultz left in his own car without saying anything to Matt.

Matt headed toward the hospital after Scott called and informed him where to go. It hadn't occurred to him until this moment that the funeral would be a great way to follow up on the missed kills by the orchestrator. That person could logically assume his targets were likely to be in that location to mourn the death of one of their members. He blamed himself for not thinking of this before. He couldn't pardon his lapse in judgment for making such a stupid mistake, and continued to curse his stupidity at not taking all possibilities into account.

He tried, without success, to justify his blunder by using Bridget's death and his grief as the reason for his blunder. *Can't do that again. Get your head in the game.* Whoever the mastermind behind these assaults was, he'd gotten Bridget and subsequently attempted to eliminate all of them. But she would be the last one of them he would murder. Matt promised himself that and added a little more.

I will kill you, whoever and wherever you are. Vengeance for Bridget will be mine. I swear it.

8

GERTI AT HOSPITAL

SCOTT PACED THE HOSPITAL FLOOR. THE NURSE TOLD HIM THE DOCTOR would be with him shortly. *Shortly, my ass. They always say that*, he realized. He hated hospitals. Spending a few days in one in Savannah, recovering from the wound received at the hand of the Russian arms dealer, had reaffirmed his intense dislike for any hospital. Now his wife had experienced some type of pregnancy trouble, and there seemed to be nothing he could do to help while they examined her.

"Mr. Donavan?" the voice came from a white-coated doctor.

"Yes?"

He led Scott into a conference room that doctors used to talk with family members away from the large waiting room area. "Your wife is doing fine. There are a couple of things about her condition that we'd like to keep an eye on. Nothing serious, but we'd like to observe her overnight.

"What's wrong with her?" Scott asked.

"Her temperature is a bit elevated, and she's complaining of muscle aches. In early pregnancy, these could be signs of an infection. We'd like to run a few tests to rule out any problems, and monitor her status."

"Can I see her?" Scott asked.

"Of course," the doctor replied, exhibiting a sympathetic smile. "I believe all will be fine with your baby." The doctor started to walk off, but turned and said, "You can visit her in her room now. Please don't stay long, though. She needs to rest."

On entering the room, Scott could see by her face that Gerti still suffered from a great deal of pain. He noticed the color was completely gone from her customary vivacious face. When she opened her eyes on his entry, she smiled at him.

"The doc says you'll be able to leave in a day. You need to rest. They want to keep you here overnight. I'll stay with you."

"No, you won't. We both know something's happening concerning the three of us. Get with Matt and figure it out. I'll be all right here. Besides, my father is sending a security team to watch out for me while I'm here. He called and said he'll be by later. Come here and kiss me and then go find out why someone's targeting us. You know how sorry I am about your sister? No one else can get hurt. Now go, and stop them."

After a brief internal struggle, Scott finally, reluctantly nodded, but kept a stern face. He waited in the room until she fell asleep and then went to the hospital café to find some coffee. Schultz called him to inform him that two security men would be arriving in a few minutes.

"Mr. Schultz, I assume your men still have the shooter. They disappeared with him, and no one at the funeral said anything about that to the police. I was—"

"Scott, let's leave it at that for now," Schultz interrupted. "I'll keep you posted."

After disconnecting, Scott returned to Gerti's room. Sitting there, he took a few deep breaths to relax, now that he knew Gerti would recover. He felt his rage at Matt start to come to the surface. He had talked to Bridget on the day of her murder and had informed her of their wedding. At that time, she had conveyed her concern that Matt might be avoiding her. She wanted to be with him, but he hadn't contacted her since their return from Savannah. Why hadn't he been with her? This thought had been boiling up in his mind since her murder.

At that moment, Matt arrived at the door to Gerti's room. *Might as well get this over with.* Scott waited a second, then moved to the entrance, and then squared off in front of Matt.

"Why the hell weren't you with Bridget?"

9

———

MATT VISITS GERTI

Taken back by Scott's confrontational comment, Matt stopped in the doorway and then stepped back a half step into the hallway. He remembered having reprimanded himself for the same thing on the drive over to the hospital, but he didn't need her brother accusing him of anything at this moment. He suffered from a personal sense of guilt, and his private grief for his tardiness in getting in contact with her. If only he hadn't delayed, she might be alive... but he knew that road led down a rabbit hole. He needed to refocus on the future, and the actions he must take to find her killer and any sponsor, if one existed. That would have to be his sole focus—find him and kill him —and maybe make him suffer.

From behind Scott, who blocked the door to bar his entrance, he heard a voice.

"Scott, what are you doing?" Gerti asked. "Matt, please come in."

Scott backed into the room and went to the opposite side of Gerti's bed.

"How are you?" Matt entered, taking careful and measured steps as he watched Scott, and then looked at Gerti.

"The doc says I'll be fine with a few days of rest."

"I'm delighted to hear that. You sure took me by surprise with your announcement at the cemetery." He moved closer to Gerti's bed and observed Scott cross his arms while his lips tightened.

"I think I shocked her father the most when I told him," Scott said, finally changing the stern face to a more congenial one.

"You got that right," Matt said. "I think Scott and I have to clear the air."

"You know he holds a doctorate and is also a true computer geek, but sometimes he…" Gerti stopped.

"I can understand how he feels," Matt interjected. "I don't doubt that you probably harbor the same question for me." Matt moved over to the window, which overlooked the parking lot a few stories below. He stared out at it for a short interval, then swung to face them with his hands behind his back.

"Your question, Scott, is the same one I have wrestled with for these past few days. Maybe if I try to explain it to you, I can manage to get it straight in my head."

"Go ahead. We're listening," Gerti said. Scott reached down and propped a pillow up behind her head.

"On my return from Savannah, I had a brain fart. I couldn't believe Bridget and I could maintain a love life and work together too. It took me two days of anguish, and then I woke up and kicked myself in the ass. What a fool I'd been. She's the greatest thing to ever happen to me. So, that morning, I went to the jeweler and bought an engagement ring." He reached into his pocket and took out a small box. He opened it and showed them the large diamond.

"I planned to ask her to marry me that night. I never got the chance." His eyes watered, and he returned his focus to the present.

"My God, that's so sweet, and so tragic," Gerti said.

"I regret that I wasn't there. I intended to be with her later that awful night." He addressed this to Scott. As he concluded, he could see Scott's posture completely soften.

"I'm sorry I attacked you like that." Scott came and stood in front of Matt, extending his hand.

Matt took it.

"I didn't realize you had such deep feelings for my sister. Your pain must be awful. She loved you too, you know."

Matt clasped his hand. "Thanks."

"We're all on the same team now. We can't change the past, but we can outline our future path. What are we going to do?" Gerti asked from her bed.

"We have to focus on the fact that someone wants the three of us dead. We need to find out who and why. Then we have to do what needs to be done," Matt said.

"You're serious?" Gerti said.

"Yes." After a few seconds, he asked Gerti, "What do you think your father would do?"

Gerti took her time before she answered. "In this case, where someone tried to kill his daughter, he would hunt them down and exterminate them. I'm starting to think like my father."

"You can't expect us to do less," Matt said.

Gerti shook her head. "I love my father, but Scott and I are going down a different path."

"What do you mean?" Matt asked.

"We have a definite future in our plans with a child on the way. We see our future home in the country, where he or she can grow up in a safe environment. That's for a start, and Father's business, with its dark side, isn't in our plans."

"You won't be taking over your dad's business?" Matt asked.

Gerti didn't respond, but Scott interjected.

"Not in our future," he said.

"Did you tell Matt about what you saw at the wine bar before the explosion?" Gerti asked.

"No, it completely slipped my mind. I'll tell him tonight. But now, we need to leave and allow you to get some rest," Scott said.

As they went out the front door of the hospital, Schultz emerged from a limo at the curb.

"Good evening, gentlemen," he said. "How is my daughter?"

"She's resting and seems to be doing fine," Scott answered.

"I've been thinking, and I want your input, Scott. I believe it would be best if we placed Gerti in a protected environment until this is resolved. We know someone is out to get you two, but I think we can protect Gerti by making her disappear."

"Not a bad idea," Matt said.

"I'm going to propose it to her now. I hope I have your support on this."

Scott nodded.

"By the way, I received information a few minutes ago from my men that the shooter has revealed something. He says all of his instructions came by email on his computer. I hear that you are something of an accomplished geek, Scott. Could you try to help us in tracking down the sender? I can't go through you, Matt, as the FBI might ask how I know this, and I don't want to go there. You understand?"

Matt nodded. "I didn't see a thing."

"Good man," Schultz said.

"I can give it a shot," Scott said to Schultz.

"It's late, and we've all had a hell of a day. Come to my hotel later. I'll give you the computer my men recovered before the locals got to his apartment. You can go to work on it. After I visit Gerti, I'll be there, but I need to return to New York tomorrow."

Schultz bade them good-bye and entered the hospital.

10

SCHULTZ VISITS HIS DAUGHTER

O*N HIS WAY TO* G*ERTI'S ROOM,* S*CHULTZ EXPERIENCED SOME TROUBLING* thoughts. The snuffing out of Bridget's life, and his daughter's close call at the hands of the sniper, had brought him a sobering realization. He could be killed at any moment, as he almost had been in Alexandria, by that nut who'd tried to blackmail him for the Bible of Constantine.

There were others who undoubtedly would like to see him gone, and his empire destroyed. Currently, he did not believe his darling daughter would be able to manage his empire at her present level of knowledge about its administration. She did not fully understand the vastness of it, and its ability to support her if he suddenly came to some unexpected end.

He wanted, with all his heart, for her to become familiar with the ins and outs of his business in order to continue to live her comfortable lifestyle, now and in the future for his expected grandchild. He needed to convince her to begin thinking about taking more responsibility for company operations. Besides, the time would soon arrive for him to semi retire. Gertrude could run the business with his diminishing involvement, and then perhaps he could even enjoy his new status as grandfather.

Schultz noticed from the doorway that Gerti appeared to be sleeping. On his entry, however, she opened her eyes. She could see him standing beside her bed in his immaculate dark blue three-thousand-dollar suit with a lighter-colored tie. With his rectangular face that showcased a strong chin, he broke into a smile when he saw her eyes open.

"Hi," he said. He lifted the flowers up for her to see.

"Thank you, Father. I'm sorry I didn't tell you about the baby earlier. It's just that everything has been crazy the last few days. We didn't find the right time. We were on the way to tell you, but the car exploded. I hope you're happy for us?"

"You're going to make me a grandfather. What do you think?" he said and smiled again. "I do wish you the same happiness with your child that I have enjoyed with you."

"Thank you."

"You know that someday, not too far in the future, you'll be taking over the business. After the two incidents where you could have been killed, I think I should arrange round-the-clock protection for you. I want you safe."

"You mean Scott and me," Gerti clarified for him. "Father, you know that I love you, but I don't want to take over your empire. Scott and I envisage a different future."

Schultz stared at her in total shock. He took his time before answering. "Of course." He decided to ignore her protests, so he moved to the other side of the bed before continuing. "I think you need to take a more businesslike approach to our enterprise. You know it's diverse and multifarious, including some things that are aboveboard and some that are not. We've always done what's necessary to protect our interests and your future. You learned that from me."

"What do you really mean?" she asked. "Is there a 'but' coming? You're about to try and outmaneuver me. I know you. You want to change my mind."

"There is a small 'but.' I think you should go into a secluded place until this current situation is resolved."

"Not without Scott," she said.

"Look at it another way. I have to shield you and the child from what I perceive as a definite danger to you. There's something going on here that we don't fully understand. Bridget Donavan was murdered. You barely escaped a bomb in New York, Matt killed an assailant, and today bullets were fired at you in the cemetery. It's best you and Scott are separated for a time."

"I don't want to. I want to be with Scott," Gerti insisted. "I also think you should consider the possibility that those shots were intended for you. You do appear to make a lot of enemies."

"I hear you, but please listen to me. I don't think that's realistic. Someone is targeting Matt and Scott, and you're in danger because you're near them. Don't you see? Someone is trying to kill them, and if you're with them, you could be a victim too."

"Wait a minute. I participated in the group that chased down the terrorist in Savannah, remember? So I could also be a target. Can't you find out who's doing this? Besides, you have a lot more resources —some, like you say, that you haven't told me about."

"I think it's time for you to hear about them. You need to be fully versed in the company you'll someday run. And that day is not too far in the future. I won't be here forever. If you'll let me, I'll put protection on you. In return, over the next few days you will learn all the firm's secrets, which I haven't shared with you before. You were always leery of hearing all the details, but I believe the time has come. Is that satisfactory?"

"No, I want to be with Scott." Gerti stared into his eyes. "We're planning to find a little house in the country, and yes, one with a white picket fence. That's the world I want—not the domain you live in."

"Are you bargaining with me?" Schultz let out a laugh. He'd counted on his daughter being the realist he knew her to be. Her future remained intertwined with her father's business, especially if she wanted to be her own person and have a secure lifestyle.

"I learned from a master," she said with a twisted grin on her face. "I don't want to, but if you insist, there can be no holding back. I have to know everything. If you die tomorrow, I realize I wouldn't be capable of handling the business. And if I'm not able to, then the future Scott and I have planned won't materialize." She knew she needed to placate him, so she sought to make it appear convincing, or there would be consequences. She consciously attempted to protect her husband. "But we will live apart from you, and I don't need to be in the business on a daily basis right now. And, all right, put me under your protection."

She watched him as he mulled this over. He always took his time in making difficult decisions. She knew that once he made up his mind, he would carry it out to the fullest. She'd inherited that quality, and now he counted on her giving up the white picket fence, at least for the present.

He stared at her. "Agreed. You go into protective custody. I'll tell you all you need to know about our business over the next few days. That's the deal you bargained for. And you don't have to take over the company on a full-time basis yet, but you must prepare to do it."

"Scott has to be part of this. Do we agree?" she pushed. "He gets to know everything."

"That wasn't in my proposal, and I don't appreciate you trying to change it."

"All right, but he can see me and visit whenever he wants?" she asked.

"Agreed," he said.

"Now, what or who do you think is attempting to kill us?" Gerti asked. "Did you come up with any ideas?"

"I don't know about you including yourself on the hit list. I think it's more about Scott and Matt."

"Why do you say that?" she asked.

"Bridget and Scott made quite a few enemies over the years. Matt's in the fray because he supported Bridget and joined forces with her. Not long ago, Scott and Bridget took out some Iranian terrorists to obtain the Crown of Thorns, and those guys have long memories. They also outwitted the Vatican by making it retract its position on the discovery of the ancient manuscripts. Bridget and

Matt killed a Russian arms dealer recently, and Scott worked with them. That's only a short list of their potential enemies. None of these involve you directly, but somehow you've managed to be in the line of fire." Taking her expression as one of concern, he continued, "Don't worry, Gertrude, I won't let anyone hurt you."

"So you're going to put all our resources behind finding out who's doing this? Notice I said 'our,' and that's the way it's going to be from now on, at your insistence. Remember, Scott and I'll need protection, if you're correct."

"I've every intention of repaying whoever did this in kind. That I promise. I just want you out of danger. Now get some rest—you've had a hectic day. We'll start our talks tomorrow."

She nodded, and her father took his leave.

* * *

Gerti stared at the closed door for a long minute after her father left. He had made some particularly insightful arguments. She would someday take over the company, but secretly she intended to eventually liquidate it. In her years of tutelage under her father about the legitimate operations the firm engaged in, he had taught her how to run that part of the business. Now, he proposed to show her all the secrets of the company. Provided it kept him happy, and peace reigned in her relationship with Scott, it would be worth playing along.

Deep in her mind, she held no aspiration to take over from her father. When and if she ended up taking over the company, she would dispose of the illegal ventures her father seemed to relish and sell the rest to fund their dreams. Scott would understand why she would have to do this in order to secure their dreams, and to be able to monetarily make their dreams come true. She felt pleased at the way she'd maneuvered her father into doing what she wanted concerning Scott. A good first step in this new world he planned to show her. She had demonstrated to him that she knew how to achieve what she desired.

She knew in the recesses of her soul that her father embraced evil, even relished it. He'd never lived the life of a good man, only one maneuvering to get what he wanted, by whatever means he needed to employ. She didn't want their child to be reared in the presence of his wickedness. She hoped she and Scott would enjoy the fruits of a happy and content life, far from the goings-on in the Schultz enterprises. Let her father continue to run the business. She would acquire the knowledge to do so if it ever became necessary, but she didn't plan on ever running her father's company in the long term.

In the end, she'd agreed to his proposal to maintain harmony between Scott and her father. Without him getting something from the negotiation, things could be fraught with discord, and downright hatred for Scott would spew forth from her father. She knew how his mind worked, and she needed to guard against hers following in the same vein. She knew that she could do exactly as her father in any circumstance, but she didn't want to do that, she had a new life now.

11

HOLY CITY OF KOM, ISLAMIC REPUBLIC OF IRAN

THE GRAND AYATOLLAH HASHAM ARAD FINISHED READING THE intelligence report. As the highest-ranking ayatollah in the country, he exercised a great deal of political authority in all matters of state. The information before him upset his normal air of calm, because of the potential ramifications if any link between Iran and the events in the reports became known.

Orders had been specific and promulgated to prevent this type of action, especially if it could be traced back to Iran. In such a case, there would be dire consequences for the Islamic religion as practiced by the Shia. His directives wouldn't have been disregarded by any of his people. He felt absolute certainty about that. The revolutionary guards, however, were another matter.

He stood up and shook his clerical robes, which made him look and feel like the true successor of the Grand Ayatollah Khomeini from the revolutionary era. His garb fell to its full length when it reached the floor as he stretched across the desk for the instrument he hated the most. The dastardly NSA's penetration of all communication devices made him reluctant in the extreme to pick up the phone. The technical people ensured him it was a safe and secure line to use. He still had reservations, but the situation demanded that he make this call.

The ayatollah stood beside his desk and waited for the president of the country to come on the phone. He disliked the man, who thought he possessed the ultimate power in the republic; the ayatollah considered him the dimwitted "Peacock President." He prided himself on knowing history, while the president didn't even know that the Shah predecessors of the current regime sat on the Peacock Throne.

After the formal greeting, the ayatollah got straight to the point of his call.

"I see Bridget Donavan is dead, murdered."

"I am aware of it," the president said.

"Mr. President, I'm concerned that some of your guards could have been involved. She did, after all, kill at least four from your personal protection unit. Someone may still want to exact vengeance for those acts." He waited for the president to speak. How the man answered might give him the clue he needed to ascertain if the man was complicit in any direct action taken against the woman.

"I assure you, I gave no such order and forbade my men from taking any actions regarding either of the Donavans. I'm fully cognizant of the threat against us if any reprisal were traced to our doorstep."

The ayatollah held his disbelief in check for the moment. The revolutionary guards had taken losses at the hands of an infidel woman. They would not soon forget that insult to their elite unit.

The original copy of the Koran—or at least they thought so—earlier found by Bridget and Scott Donavan now resided in the Vatican. That document might contain the necessary scripture passages to prove that the Shia branch of Islam represented the true line of succession of the Prophet. The Roman pontiff had sequestered those documents in the papal archives, and through proxy contacts, he had conveyed a direct threat to the Islamic Republic of Iran.

A Swiss diplomat had verbally delivered the message from the Roman pontiff months ago. Short and straight to the point: "Any attack by any person or persons of Iran against the persons of Bridget or Scott Donavan will result in those scriptures being lost to Islam forever." None but the highest levels of the government were privy to this communication from the Vatican.

"As a precaution, I intend to send feelers out to all our contacts in America to ascertain if any of your people or my people were involved in the murder. Some renegade, believing he is doing a good deed for our country, is always a possibility. I want to make sure nothing can be traced back to us."

The ayatollah reasoned that if the Shia branch of Islam acquired the scriptures before the Sunni, then they would control the release and interpretation of the manuscript. If those documents went against their positions in some fundamental manner, then a judicious correction could be applied before the world became aware of the actual text.

As long as the pope possessed the manuscripts, that couldn't happen. And as yet, they had failed to formulate a usable idea on gleaning the pope's intentions regarding the use of those documents.

"I'll do the same for my people, but I want you to stay away from any contact with my revolutionary guard, Grand Ayatollah. Be clear on that point," the president said before he hung up.

12

SCOTT AT HOSPITAL

SCOTT ARRIVED AT THE HOSPITAL BEFORE BREAKFAST. HE FERRIED TWO coffees and cinnamon raisin bagels. He entered Gerti's room, where he held out his morning offering.

"So thoughtful. That'll be so much better than the bland breakfast they provided." She pointed at the untouched food on the rolling tray table beside her bed.

"How are you feeling today?" He bent over and gave her a kiss on the cheek.

"Fine. Father stopped by last night before returning to New York. I believe he beamed with delight when you told him he would soon be a grandfather," Gerti said.

"What did he have to say?" Scott asked. He sat on the side of Gerti's bed holding her hand.

"We sort of went over the possibilities concerning who might be behind these attacks. All four of us were targeted on the same night, and then that sniper at the cemetery. There has to be a common thread. Father suggested that perhaps it might be Iranian terrorists, He also thought the Russians were a possibility, and the last thing he mentioned concerned the Vatican. You and Bridget did deceive them during the adventure to recover the crown, and then there was the problem she caused with the Bibles of Constantine fiasco."

"I don't think he left anyone out." Scott smiled as he realized how long the list of their enemies had become. "What do you think?"

"We need to develop a plan. There's no way we can check on the Islamic terrorists, but you know that Vatican priest, right? Why don't you give him a call and see if you can glean anything on that front? Also, there's that man, Val, in Russia, who saved us during that gun battle on our trip to St. Petersburg to learn about the icon. Might be a good idea if I call him. I think he liked me."

"That call can wait for a few days, this is rest time for you."

"Pushy are we, dear husband?" She gave him a coquettish smile indicating she didn't buy it. "I also agreed to go into Father's protective environment. You will come to visit me often, won't you?" She pouted as she said this.

"You bet I will. I'm glad you concurred with your father. I'll feel much better knowing you're safe until this is over. We all understand that the real goal here is to protect all of our lives."

"One more thing," she said.

He stopped drinking his coffee and waited for her to continue.

"Father wants me to prepare to take over his company."

"What? We agreed that wasn't going to be the course we took."

"I know, but we've got to be realistic. That's where the funding for our dreams is going to come from. I want you to be with me on this, so we can run it together. I believe it's the only sure way we'll be able to enjoy a rich future. It's the best deal I could make."

She expected him to say something, but he shook his head and huffed out of the room without saying another word.

He called her on his way home. "I'm sorry for the way I acted. I just thought we'd agreed on our plans for down the road, and you changed them without even discussing it with me."

"If you would've given me a chance to explain, then you might not feel so betrayed. I didn't change our plan," Gerti said. "You must remember that I negotiated with Father. I merely explained to you what took place with him. I needed to give something to get something."

"What did you give?"

"I told him he could instruct me in all the things I don't know about the company. There can't be that many, as I've been almost running the day-to-day operations over the last year or so anyway. He wants to know that I'll be taken care of if he passes without warning."

"What did you get out of it?" Scott asked.

"I got us freedom. Without this agreement, he could make our married life miserable. Believe me, he could. You and he seem to get along now, and I didn't want to see him start to treat you in a different manner. So, by saying that he could tell me all the trade secrets, I kept peace in the family. I harbor no intention of taking over the firm in the way he envisions. We'll make our own future, I promise."

* * *

AT LUNCHTIME, SCOTT RETURNED TO HIS APARTMENT AND EXAMINED the computer he'd received from Schultz. He wondered what had happened to the man who'd shot at them in the cemetery, but that remained a minor concern to him. He would start on the laptop after he made a phone call. He dug out the cell number for Monsignor Jonathan McGregor in Rome, and soon he heard a deep voice with a slight Scottish accent.

"Hello, Bridget. What a surprise to hear from you."

Scott realized the name displayed from his phone to the priest's must show "Donavan." Bridget herself always called the Vatican.

"Jonathan, this is Scott."

"Oh, hello, Scott. How are you?"

"Listen, I bear some bad news. I'll come out and say it. Bridget is dead."

"My God. I'm so sorry. What happened?"

"She was murdered. And about the time of Bridget's attack, someone also attacked Gerti and me in New York, and Matt Higgins in Alexandria, Virginia. The rest of us were lucky enough to survive, but Bridget wasn't. A lone attacker butchered her. She died after killing her murderer."

"You sound like you believe it to be an orchestrated assault," McGregor said.

"Again, I'll be direct. Does the Vatican have us in their sights? Are we targeted by someone there because of our connection to the Crown of Thorns or the Bible of Constantine?"

"Absolutely not." The volume of the denial caused Scott to take the phone from his ear. He reseated it on the other side of his head.

"No, really. I'm sure we pissed off some high-ranking member of the church with some of our actions. Is there anyone who would be after revenge? The Catholic Church has been known to go after someone categorized as an enemy." Scott waited for a response.

"I hear what you're saying, but I do believe you're barking up the wrong tree. You and Bridget did cause a few inconveniences to Rome by some of your acts, but that pales in comparison to your other recent ventures. Those involves with any of them might have taken out a contract on you. I assure you it isn't the Vatican. I'll put out feelers, but I'm in a position here to know of anything like a Papal hit."

"Thank you."

"Accept my condolences, and I will pray for the soul of my friend Bridget."

* * *

JONATHAN PLACED THE PHONE ON HIS DESK. HIS MIND BOGGLED BECAUSE of this news. Bridget dead. What a tragedy. What a loss of a beautiful person. He didn't believe anyone at the Vatican could be involved.

He went over to his small refrigerator in the apartment overlooking the dome of St. Peters and withdrew a beer. After pouring it into a glass, he returned and sat on his sofa. The lights illuminating the basilica shone brilliant against the clear night sky. He knew about the pope's diplomatic message to the Iranians, which had been delivered right after Rome recanted its position on the crown and Bible affairs. That, in his mind, eliminated them from the mix of possible assassins.

The idea that someone in the Vatican would endeavor to kill either of them seemed preposterous. He sipped his beer. The one thing Scott and Bridget had accomplished consisted of revealing some of the manuscripts they'd found in the Warsaw museum without getting the Vatican's permission. That didn't warrant the type of reaction Scott had described. Their actions had broken their agreement with Rome, but he knew the exact circumstances that had precipitated those actions, and he understood why they did it. Still...

He picked up the phone and dialed the ancient curator in the Vatican Museum, Monsignor Richard Potter-Cogan, whose tentacles stretched everywhere in Rome. Many years before, the old priest had been Jonathan's philosophy professor; Jonathan's love of Aristotle and the polemics had permanently endeared him to his mentor. Jonathan explained to the monsignor his concerns that some of the Agnus Dei Society might be engaged in some unsanctioned activities in America.

"I suppose it's possible. Some of these new warrior-priests are adamant in their belief in the Agnus Dei group. I'll do some investigating and get back to you soon. Goodnight, Jonathan."

He next called Captain Grossman of the Swiss Guards and made the same appeal to him, receiving the identical assurance of an inquiry.

As the special assistant to the Vatican secretary of state, Jonathan enjoyed access to almost everything that transpired in the Vatican. He would use that privilege to delve into this matter on his own. It was possible someone here in the Vatican might bear a grudge against the Donavans.

It seemed highly unlikely, but one never knew, he thought.

One never knew.

13

ST. PETERSBURG, RUSSIA

The man paced the marble floor of his elaborate mansion situated against a mountain backstop, with a frontal view facing the sea. The weather remained unseasonably warm for the autumn, and he enjoyed leaving the windows open to let the salt air blow through the upstairs of the house. He had purchased this residence a few months ago. The primary reason for the purchase entailed the magnificent scene provided by the vast expanse of the ocean waters of the Baltic that could be viewed from his veranda.

He gave up on trying to reach the man whom he had contracted to do the hits in the States. That man supposedly handled the details of the ten-million-dollar contract. Initially, he'd intended to carry out on his own vendetta in America against the person who killed his nephew, but now his new client paid for the expenses in an operation he'd been hoping to conduct for some time. His only problem was that he didn't know the identity of the individual who murdered his relative. He hoped this current job might provide him with the information he sought.

For each contract, he used email as his only method for communication with his contact in the States. The man's identity remained hidden behind numerous firewalls and various servers placed at specific points around the world. Right now, he felt blind. He knew things had gone south on the first effort to eliminate all three targets, but he needed to get his man to finish it, and do it in short order.

The agreement with his single point of contact in America, he learned, had been subcontracted out to three different agents over there. Two of those men were now dead, and the ones hired for the New York job appeared to have been eliminated for their failure, probably by the man he contracted. The last message he'd received, now two days old, said his contact would solve the problem at a funeral. No communication since then. On entering his office on the second floor, he went to his computer and looked for any word from America.

No new email greeted him on the machine.

His private cell rang. "Out of Area" appeared. This could be one of his men, hopefully calling to say they'd obtained some news through their contacts.

"You blathering fool," the Robocop voice said.

Before he answered, he managed to control his shock at his caller's greeting.

"You couldn't even handle a simple contract," the voice said.

"Wait. It will be completed. My man in the States assures me he'll finish the job." He needed to appease the caller who, by his initial deposit, remained entitled to results. He didn't want to give the money back. He had never done that in his life.

"You only succeeded on one of the targets. If this is not finished quickly, you will not receive the rest of your money. These have to be clean hits."

"There will be no collateral damage. One third of our arrangement has been completed. The rest will be shortly."

"Make it so, or you yourself will pay," the computer-generated voice answered him with.

He hung up the phone with a smile on his face. In his mind, that bordered on a stupid thing to say, especially from someone who couldn't possibly reach him. After doing his research, and with the technical experts at his disposal, he'd learned who the voice belonged to. Two could play at this game, he mused. He could do damage to the one who employed him anytime he needed to. His smile stretched across his face. He would never work with someone he didn't know and who he couldn't eliminate if that became necessary. His technical people knew how to backtrack a phone call. Yes, after this was over, he might make the bastard pay for talking to him in such a manner, and acting like a buffoon with the altered voice tactic.

He glanced in admiration at the two beautiful Petro Aivazovsky paintings on the wall of his office, and the idyllic maritime scenes brought solace to his weary soul. "The Snowstorm" and "The Sixth Wave" lifted his heart on seeing such beauty and grace, captured in an instant of time and made immortal by the artist's hand. He grinned for a second. He thought of himself as an artist too, and decided that his brush would, in due course, paint Robocop off the face of the earth.

14

SCHULTZ AT HOME

SCHULTZ SIPPED HIS DALMORE SCOTCH WHILE HE WATCHED THE radiant sunset over Central Park. This view always held his interest, ever since the first day he'd witnessed the spectacle subsequent to purchasing his penthouse. He enjoyed the peacefulness of the moment, even relished it, as he stood on his balcony overlooking the park facing west. At least his daughter was now in a safe place. His security men reported every two hours and would continue to do so until midnight, and then only if something changed before six in the morning.

His thoughtful serenity dissipated when the cell phone buzzed. He walked over to the ringing instrument. He saw the number of the interrogation team displayed.

"Yes?" he said and waited.

"Mr. Schultz, the man has given us an email address. He says it's the only way he ever communicated with the person who hired him for the hit. I believe our persuasion has loosened his tongue a bit, but we're no experts at this."

Shultz pondered this for a moment before he answered, "Good work. Send me the information he gave you and continue. I want everything out of him."

"Yes, sir."

Schultz hung up the receiver and took a moment to collect his thoughts. He now possessed something he could use. He called Scott to give him the information.

"Please concentrate on that email address now that you have that computer. I hope you can trace it."

Shultz had some doubts that Scott could do anything, but he supposed he must let him try because Gertrude thought him to be a computer nerd.

"Give me a few hours, and I'll get back to you," Scott said.

* * *

SCOTT SAT IN HIS ALEXANDRIA, VIRGINIA, APARTMENT AND BOOTED UP the computer he had received from Schultz. His little office area had a view that looked out on the Potomac River. The place didn't have any luxury items, but he had outfitted it with furniture from Ikea, and since renting it, he had spent very little time here.

Backtracking an email was usually considered child's play to him. Once he located the address on the computer, it shouldn't be too difficult to trace it. Having the exact address, he believed, would materially reduce the time it would require.

The laptop lacked a password for him to have to crack— a very stupid omission, Scott knew. He found there were two thousand emails in the inbox. The guy, a certifiable packrat, must have never cleaned it out. Focusing on the target address, he went to work. He noticed there were only three with the specific address that he searched for in the files, and he carefully read each one.

The first laid out a contract to hit him, Matt and Bridget. The sum of one million dollars would be paid for the hits to be carried out concurrently. The second contained a blistering reprimand for not executing all the targets simultaneously, and a condemnation of the man's efforts. The email concluded with a threat to kill the man if the contract remained incomplete by the time of the funeral. The third, received just two days ago, requested information on the completion of the kills.

Backtracking where the messages had been sent from took more time than Scott had originally estimated. They had been routed through numerous servers in various locations around the world. The sender had taken extreme precautions to ensure no one could easily find his location. Backtracking to the original IP address would be more difficult than he'd initially imagined—perhaps even impossible.

Never mind, I'll get you, thought Scott, and he dove into the project to prove to Mr. Schultz that he could do it. After three hours, he took a break and examined his findings. He'd been able to narrow it down to a vague point of origin, but the date he'd extracted was insufficient; he realized he'd need more sophisticated software to pinpoint an exact location. The layers of protection used to hide the sender's identity were far more complex than the average person would have access to, but he felt pretty sure of his initial findings on the sender's general location.

He sent the recovered emails to Schultz and then made a call.

* * *

IN A SMALL FARMHOUSE EAST OF STAUNTON, VIRGINIA, KARIM PAHLAVI sat watching television in his bedroom. The windows were barred, and the single door into his room remained locked from the outside. Beyond that door, Karim knew two FBI special agents stood guard. On more than one occasion, he had observed another agent outside, walking around the grounds of the house.

They usually deprived him of sleep, played loud music, gave him short rations, and anything else the sadistic guard named Ken could think of to torment him.

"We're going to send you to Gitmo, or better yet, to some dark site in Saudi, where you'll talk." This agent had a horrible personality. They didn't realize that he didn't know anything to tell them. He'd pretended that he knew some hidden secrets that he wouldn't reveal, but in reality, he had little to give them—just some bits of info that would be old by now. At some point in time, they would realize it and send him off to some prison, or worse, where the conditions would be far less pleasant than this farmhouse. At least here, he felt safe, if isolated.

On a normal night, he would be in front of some interrogator attempting to extract information on the arms-dealing network that supplied homegrown terrorists in the States. They sometimes denied him any television for days, but today they somehow were generous. He relished getting some news about the world.

On the screen, a reporter commented on the brutal murder of a female in Alexandria, Virginia. They showed a picture of the victim. Karim's heart jumped. The bitch had received her just reward. He couldn't believe it, Bridget Donavan dead. Matt Higgins, the FBI agent who worked with her, was not mentioned, but they covered the fact that Bridget Donavan's brother had suffered an attempt on his life the same night. The FBI now searched for the mastermind behind these attacks. They were appealing to the public to provide any information on the cases.

Karim remembered his effort to kill Higgins, and the aftermath, when he had fallen captive to the man. He hadn't completed his mission because of an unfortunate turn of events. That misadventure had become his undoing in the arms trade for which he had received specialized training in Iran. There he had learned how to work with arms dealers and also developed the ability to conduct that type of business by himself. He now sat in silence, contemplating what he might be able to do with this delightful new information. There must be a way to employ it, to get him freed from his confinement by the FBI. He started developing the incipient concept of a plan. He realized that to capitalize on it, he needed to act, and do it now, while this news was fresh.

He now believed this serendipitous newscast presented a unique opportunity to gain his freedom. The FBI used the threat of labeling him an enemy combatant so they could hold him forever. He hadn't told them anything yet, but this news might contain the chip he could employ in the strategy he started to concoct in his mind.

As a starting point in his new scheme, he could offer up his contacts in the Iranian Revolutionary Guard operating in the States. In addition, he could provide limited information on his association with the Russian arms dealers. Now the time to play that chip had arrived.

He went over to the door and knocked.

"What do you want?" came the voice of the FBI guard.

"I'm ready to talk, but only to FBI Special Agent Matt Higgins."

15

EMAIL TRACED TO RUSSIA

MATT HIGGINS ANSWERED HIS CELL ON THE FIRST RING.

"What have you got, Scott?"

"I think I've found the point of origin for the email to the man Schultz has. I believe it's somewhere in Russia. I know you don't want to use FBI assets on this unless absolutely necessary."

"No, I don't. I want to keep this off-book as much as possible like the director ordered," Matt said. After a few seconds he added, "So it's not Iran? I remember you told me about the Iranians you saw in the wine bar before the explosion. Have you relayed anything about this to Schultz?"

"I did send him the emails I found on the computer. I also copied you. I thought you might like to know this ASAP. I'll tell him about Russia. I don't want him going off half-cocked because I can't swear on a stack of Bibles that I absolutely know the location. You hear me, I don't know for sure. So don't you get too excited. I didn't obtain a specific IP address of a computer or any definite physical place at this time. I'm still working on it, but that's my initial best estimate. It'll take me more time to confirm it."

Matt thanked him and hung up. Russia? At least not Iran and

those radical jihadist nuts. In a flash, he came up with the germ of an idea. A far-fetched one, but he didn't have anything else. Sitting around and thinking about Bridget would eventually eat him up. He decided not to go down that road, but to get payback instead. *Do something*, he told himself. *Even if it ends up being wrong, get out there and try.*

* * *

MATT TOOK A CALL FROM LIZ GARCIA. SHE WANTED TO ARRANGE A meeting between him and a man well known to him, Karim. This came as a total surprise. Matt knew one person with a working knowledge of a possible suspect in Russia and maybe even Iran—Karim. What a coincidence to receive a call from Liz about the man. Karim might be useful if Russia turned out to be the focal point of interest. At least Matt would be doing something. Liz told him when and where to be for the meeting.

On arrival at the FBI safe house, Matt observed Karim as he sat with his hands shackled to a table in a room like any detention cell, with a mirror and a video camera. The man wore a blue denim shirt and pants. His unkempt beard hid most of his face, but couldn't hide his prominent nose. Meanwhile, his black eyes radiated intelligence and also conveyed a high degree of hatred toward anyone who might sit across from him.

The terrorist, Karim, was currently being held in this FBI safe house for a "debriefing" after the shoot-out with Matt and Bridget in Savannah. The original director's idea concerning Karim entailed breaking this man down to get the information they needed to destroy other homegrown terrorist cells operating on American soil. So far they had produced no results after an extended time.

This man had previously enjoyed contact with many different units operating in the States before he had taken over the cell that Matt and Bridget had decimated at the Port of Savannah. In that city, Karim had attempted without success to steal a container of weapons from a Russian arms dealer named Michael Alexandrovitch.

Matt presented a plan to the FBI director on his way to see Karim. The head of the FBI didn't like the idea. He thought it might involve too much freedom for Karim. Matt assured him that Karim would be under constant surveillance if the director allowed him to implement his idea. The director reluctantly agreed and conceded that it might be a somewhat viable option, if it worked. He left it up to Matt to decide if he wanted to implement the course of action as outlined.

Matt stared at Karim through a two-way mirror. Two new intelligence agents from the CIA and the DIA stood at his side. It was their first visit to see Karim, and both were interested in any information the man could provide concerning ongoing operations against any target in the homeland or abroad. So far they had come up empty, as Karim continued to be uncooperative.

"What do you know about this asshole?" CIA asked. "We read his file, but you have firsthand experience with him."

"To sum it up for you," Matt said, "he was born in Iran twenty-nine years ago. That's years after the great revolution under the Grand Ayatollah Khomeini. His grandparents were arrested and executed by the revolutionary guards of Khomeini because of their wealth, and also because of their Western education and contacts. His parents survived by going underground. In secret, they taught him the ways of the West. On his tenth birthday, his mother and his father were caught by the authorities, not because of any action on their part, but because this scumbag turned them in for anti-revolutionary writings."

"Did that get his mother and father killed?" DIA interjected. "None of this is in the file."

"No, it's not. I haven't had time to do a full debrief since Savannah. That's why I'm doing this recap. Yes, his parents suffered the same fate. Karim went to a religious school to study the Koran and become a good Muslim. The days of the brutality of the revolution were past, and he appeared as no threat after turning his own parents in." Matt took a pause in the narrative.

"He's a real piece of work. How did he get involved in the training of terrorists?" CIA asked. "We'll need to put this information in his file."

"He became an asset for them because he spoke good English, since his parents had taught him from birth in that language, and because he exhibited an aptitude for spy craft. Are you guys going to try and use him?" Matt asked.

"No. We're here to obtain background on him from you, if possible. We understand you arrested him for operations on U.S. soil, and we realize that's the FBI's business. Thanks for the briefing. So you know, we obtained his picture and prints. We'll fill in his jacket with the detailed info you've provided," said the CIA agent.

They shook hands, and the agents departed.

Matt continued to observe Karim. He couldn't put all the pieces of any future plan together just yet.

Matt understood that his primary mission focused on finding out who had targeted them. Bridget's death still plagued him every waking moment. Someone would pay for that. In a discussion with Gerti and Scott, the possibilities seemed centered on the Russians, the Iranians, and even the Catholic Church.

Bridget had shot the nephew of a Russian mobster in Savannah, and now she was dead. Matt thought that the Russian might be the most obvious culprit. He could guess, but he had nothing solid to go on. But on the other hand, she had killed a few Iranian terrorists in her hunt for the Crown of Thorns. So this scheme he had conjured up might provide some answers—but he would need Karim, the lying, conniving bastard, to be involved.

Matt's idea was that, if Russia was the source of their troubles, Karim might have criminal contacts in Russia. He had met with the nephew of Alexandrovitch before his death, but it would be premature to involve Karim at this stage of his operation. The burning question remained: what scheme fomented in Karim's mind? He had asked for this meeting. He must want something—his freedom, obviously, but that wasn't Matt's to give.

On viewing the man through the mirror, he felt like bashing his face in. He knew he could never trust Karim, but he thought he might be able to employ him in the future in his yet-to-be-fully-developed plan of action. At their last encounter, Karim had deceived Matt into thinking Karim had become an asset for the FBI, and then he'd turned against him, almost killing him. So when the director had raised the question of security concerning Karim, Matt had quickly responded, "Sir, if he agrees to work with us and then blinks, or tries to change the agreement, I'll personally kill him."

His anger rose in his chest on the thought that this dirt bag might be of some use in finding Bridget's murderer, but he might as well take advantage of the opportunity to face the man. He needed to confirm that Karim held some of the essential elements of his yet incomplete concept. He moved toward the entrance and flung the door open.

"Hello, Karim," he said as he entered the room. "I'm going to kill you."

* * *

KARIM FLIPPED HIS HEAD BACK AS MATT'S FIST SWISHED BY HIS FACE, missing it by an inch.

He is really angry, Karim realized. *There has to be more to his presence than that, though, and maybe I can use it to my advantage. Stick to the plan*, he reminded himself.

"They told me you wanted to see me. To what do I owe this honor?" Matt said in a controlled voice.

Karim would not let Matt see the fear he had in his gut displayed on his face.

"First off, I want to say that I regret that you made it out of Savannah alive," Matt said. He took a seat in the chair opposite and seemed to be watching for Karim's reaction. Karim decided to change tactics a bit and show a little fear, so he moved back in the seat and scrunched his shoulders as he lowered his eyes.

"But I have always liked you. I didn't kill you when I was ordered to," Karim offered.

"That's because I stopped you and captured you," Matt said. "So, I assume you're here to get something from me, or to persuade me to do something for you."

Karim looked into Matt's eyes without blinking. He decided to wait for some type of answer.

Matt didn't speak for a whole minute, and then he said, "Are you aware that Bridget Donavan is dead?"

"I'm in custody, not seclusion. Yes, I know that," Karim answered for the first time. He almost smiled, but caught himself. He needed to play this cool, even to be subservient if required to get the man to ask him for something that would allow an obligation to be incurred.

"I do believe that some people from her past came after her. Do you know anything about this?"

"I hear you. You want information from me, but there must be something in this for me. If I help you, can I get out of this place?" Anywhere else, he might escape, but not from a twenty-four-hour confinement. "Otherwise, I see no motive to tell you anything. I'm looking at Guantanamo or some other fed site for years to come, according to the FBI guards."

"Yes, you are," Matt said, and he took his time before again speaking again. "Maybe I can do something about that."

"I think I'll require more than your word." Karim decided to push a little to receive some type of assurance that his help would provide him some leniency, at least in the short term.

"No, you don't, because you don't get anything else, and this might be your one chance. Got that?" Matt went over and unplugged the security camera hanging on the wall that was recording the interview. He returned and slammed his fist on the table in front of Karim. Karim saw that Matt had hatred in his eyes, and he felt the anger radiating from the man, ready to explode.

Karim started to fear in earnest that the man might try to kill him. "Now that we have complete privacy, and from your actions I see that we're off the record, what can I do for you?" Karim placed a smile on his face that stretched from chin to forehead.

"I need information on who might have put a hit out on her," Matt said. "You told the guards you'd talk to me. So talk."

"Well, for your word that you'll assist me in getting out of here…"

"I didn't say anything about getting you out of here," Matt interrupted. "I said I might be able to help you."

"I'll take you at your word." He decided to give something to get into the man's favor in order to get something in return. He didn't have any sure-fire bargaining chips. All his connections to the Revolutionary Guards and to the Russian arms dealers were now dormant, so why not tell him something he might want to hear? "Before the problems I had in Savannah, I heard rumors from some of my Iranian contacts that the Revolutionary Guards were pissed at the Donavans and were planning to take some type of action against them."

"What type of action?" Matt asked.

"How should I know? I'm here in this fake prison. Get me out where I can make some contacts, and I can discover more. It's the best I can offer from in here."

"No, it's not. As far as we could determine, you didn't maintain any communication with your Iranian handler for months. So, you're full of shit. I'm wasting my time here." Matt stood up, preparing to leave.

"No, no. Please, I do maintain some connections in the Guards and I could find out more."

Matt moved closer to the door.

"Matt, wait a minute. The other possibility is the Russians. You know I have acquaintances there. I met many of the Russki arms dealers during my travels around with some of the American cells. I also made contact with Mike Alexandro in Savannah on a few occasions, and his higher-ups know who I am. I can access them, but not from in here. They wouldn't even know that you arrested me—they'll just think I got away and went into hiding."

"You'd say anything to get out of this place." Matt stopped his progress to the exit, however, and refocused on Karim.

"I speak the truth. I have contacts with the Russians, and they know me," Karim insisted. He needed Matt to believe him, to need his help.

"Can you still get in touch with them?" Matt queried.

"Yes."

"Don't go anywhere." Matt smiled as he left the room.

16

MATT SUMMONED TO NEW YORK

Matt received a call from Schultz a few minutes after leaving Karim. He answered it, expecting to hear news about the Russian connection Scott uncovered. Schultz didn't waste time on pleasantries.

"Matt, would it be possible for you to come to New York? I want you to question the man my men captured at the cemetery. I brought him up here so I could, shall we say, supervise the questioning."

This took Matt by surprise. What type of interrogation did Schultz have in mind? He wanted to be involved in Schultz's "questioning," because he needed all the information the sniper might possess.

"I'm sure your men are good at extraction techniques." He sought to determine the motivation behind Schultz's request.

Schultz seemed to hesitate before he commented. "Yes, but I believe you're better trained than my men at this type of work. Mine haven't learned much. Not sure they're the right people for this job. Don't you want to participate?"

"I'll be on the next flight. Should I come to your apartment?"

"No, I'll text you the address."

Matt wrestled with the problem of someone other than the FBI questioning the suspect. Schultz's men had captured the guy, and no evidence existed to point law enforcement to where the man had been taken. They assumed he had gotten away. The director might not like this, but Matt followed his gut. Bridget's death erased any doubts—he might need to do some things that would bother him, but he knew he would do them anyway. Whatever he needed to do to find her killers would be worth it if Bridget's death would be avenged. Even thinking of her caused a visceral reaction. He missed her. He'd been a fool. Now he would make it up to her, even though it would only be to her memory.

Hatred for the killer boiled in his blood. He headed for Reagan International to catch the next shuttle to New York.

Matt arrived at the address supplied by Schultz and paid the taxi. He went inside the dilapidated building on Long Island. Its red brick construction predated WWII. A smell permeated the place. The aroma reminded him of the stink emanating from dead camels he'd passed by in the Middle East during combat operations. Matt guessed, from some of the lingering fragrances, it used to be a leather-conditioning factory. On the plane ride, he'd wracked his brain about what to do in the coming hours. He could learn much about Bridget's killing from this man, but he hated the shooter with a vengeance before he even entered the building.

"Matt, over here," he heard Schultz call for him.

"I want to check up on my life insurance coverage before going any further in here." He gave Schultz a warm smile as he said this. "I hope this isn't one of your investments."

"I assure you, this building will soon be worth a fortune," Schultz said as he shook Matt's hand. "Follow me."

On approaching a dingy room filled with the remnants of leather leftovers from the industrial plant, Matt wanted to take out his hand-kerchief to cover his nose.

"Has he given any more information?" Matt asked.

"No. Just that he received all his instructions from the email address he gave us. But somehow I don't believe that. He would have maintained some contact with his employer, if for no other reason than that the employer would want to monitor him. At least, that's what I'm thinking," Schultz said.

"What are your men doing?" Matt asked before they entered the room.

"Roughing him up. I'm not a big fan of torture," Schultz said with a wink, "but I like it better than my daughter being dead. You know this animal is responsible for Bridget's death. He has the info we need to get the man who ordered the hits. I think it's worth inflicting a little pain to find out who. Can you handle this?"

Without waiting on an answer, Schultz pushed open the door. Matt observed a man hanging from chains with his toes barely touching the floor. With the hatred he felt overflowing into his mind, Matt walked over to where the man hung and gave him a vicious right cross.

"That's for starters," Matt said. "I'm here to ask you a few questions. These others can leave now." He looked in Schultz's direction, and the man signaled for his men to depart with a shake of his head.

Matt again approached to within striking distance of the man. "What's your name?" When he received no response, his right fist connected to the man's jaw with a bone-crushing impact. *I now have a chance to find out who is responsible for killing Bridget. I'm willing to do anything to find out a name.*

The man spat at him. "I won't talk to you."

Matt again punched him.

"What's your name?" Matt repeated.

After Schultz and his men closed the door behind them, Matt saw the man raise his head. He appeared ready to say something.

"John," he whispered as blood ran down from his nose. The man smiled at Matt. "Are you here to sweet-talk me?"

Matt again started to bash him in the face but said, "I don't want to keep doing this, but I have to know who paid you to kill us."

Twelve hours passed as Matt attempted to get the man to give up more information on who had hired him. In the morning, Matt felt exhausted. He wasn't getting anywhere with the sniper. He needed to take a different tack. Physical pain hadn't worked.

"I'm going to inject you with a truth drug. Then we'll find out who paid you." Matt didn't know if they really possessed anything like truth serum to use on the man, but bluffing seemed like a reasonable idea right now. No response.

He stepped back from the man as Schultz's two men entered the room and stared at the sniper, nodding their approval on seeing the condition of the victim.

After waiting a few minutes, Matt moved in close to look in the man's eyes. They didn't focus on him. The man appeared barely on the edge of consciousness. "Who hired you to do the hits? Where is he?" Matt demanded for the umpteenth time.

Schultz came into the room. "Matt, ease up. Calm down a bit. If I'd wanted him dead, my men could have handled that. We need information. Any progress?"

"Nothing more." Matt looked at the sniper and shouted, "Who hired you?"

The response came as a glare of hatred from the man.

"It's time to give him a truth drug. You mentioned that you have a doctor somewhere nearby. Can we get him to help?"

"Of course." Schultz dialed his phone and said into it, "Come now."

Matt moved beside Schultz where he addressed the man. "This is your last chance. Once the doctor gives you a shot that will make you talk. For the last time, who hired you?" Matt didn't know if they possessed anything like truth serum to use on the man or if what they had would make him talk or kill him.

Matt took the opportunity to go to the restroom, relieve himself, and throw water on his face. After ten minutes, he returned to the room. Schultz's men had inflicted more damage on the man hanging from the ceiling. They continued to pummel the sniper without respite for some minutes. Schultz waited for a few more minutes, and then he picked up a paper cup, filled it with water from the faucet, and took it over to the sniper.

"Drink this," Schultz said. "You must be conscious to answer the questions. You don't want to be punished any more, so why don't you give us the name of the one who hired you?"

The man, his face battered, with a crusted-shut left eye and blood draining from multiple hits to his head, somehow nodded.

"He's at the Vatican," the man said in an audible mumble, scarcely discernable.

"What?" shouted Matt. "You're full of shit."

"He's in the Vatican," the sniper whispered again, and his eyes lost focus as his head dropped to his chest.

"Shit," was the sole word that came from Matt.

"Get the doc in here," Schultz ordered his men. He faced Matt and said, "He's been on my payroll for years. Knows how to not talk."

From another door, one of the Schultz's men led a small, hunched-over ancient man into the room. The silver-haired doc carried a black bag seen on many doctors who make house calls. The physician approached the victim, taking his pulse and examining his eyes. He then looked at Schultz.

"I have to give him some morphine to relieve his pain, and you must let him rest. He's barely alive."

He gave the man an injection, then picked up his kit and departed. In less than a minute, Matt watched as the man went into violent convulsions. He jerked back and forth trying to free his arms from the restraints and flipped his head into an extreme contorted position.

Schultz stared at the scene but didn't move.

Matt approached the limp man and checked for a pulse. He found none.

17

———

MATT AFTER CONDUCTING INTERROGATION

OUTSIDE, AFTER HE WATCHED THE MAN DIE, MATT FELT PERSONAL failure. He had participated in torture, knowing he shouldn't have, but it had achieved a result. The doc couldn't save the sniper, and now there remained the statement by the dying man that his contract for the killings came from someone connected with the Vatican. Matt's mind told him this information contained the lead they needed to follow. He had obtained nothing else concrete to go on, but he had a dead man's confession.

Bridget had repeatedly told him that she'd made peace with the Vatican on all counts, but then again, maybe they hadn't made it with her. There existed one obvious motive—revenge—and that might be a reason for someone there to take action against the Donavans. The man, when he'd broken, had conveyed certainty about who had hired him. There was no reason for him to lie in his condition, nor with his last breath.

Schultz came up behind him, patted him on the back, and walked him to the car.

"What's on your mind?" Schultz asked.

Matt thought he should arrest Schultz and turn himself in, but he needed to get to the bottom of this. He stopped and faced Schultz.

"We have a dying man who told us that someone at the Vatican is the culprit we're after. I think I need to go over there and find out who could have ordered these attacks. It's the only clue we've obtained about the perpetrator of these assaults."

"My primary concern is to get this solved. I can send a team to take out whomever you find responsible," Schultz said.

"We need more information as to the specific target," Matt said. "I'd like to be on my way to Rome tomorrow to run this lead down, and to take whatever action I deem necessary to avenge Bridget."

"Wait a second. Let me provide you with my plane. It'll be my pleasure, and it'll get you where you need to go on your own schedule. You're going to be helping my daughter by your actions, so take it."

Matt shook his hand and said they would be ready to go in the morning if the plane could be in D.C. to pick them up. Schultz nodded.

Matt took the next shuttle back, and when he arrived at his Alexandria apartment, he found Scott waiting there for him.

"What's up?" Matt asked.

"When I called you to ask you if I could meet you here, I told you that I had a tentative location of the email sender. I needed to get in touch with an old friend of mine, a superb hacker, in order to acquire better software than what I have. He uses TOR."

"What the hell is TOR?" Matt asked.

"Later. You won't believe it, but he's a hacker from the university where I worked. He befriended me while I taught there, and always thought I got screwed by the way they fired me. So he helped me on some previous occasions with computer problems. We did some coding together. Anyway, I contacted him, and he sent me one of his programs that can go deeper into tracking the origins of emails than anything I have."

"So what did you find?" Matt injected. "Just tell me. Then I've got some news for you."

"The software led me from the initial position in Russia to a new location somewhere in the city of Rome," Scott said.

Matt stared at him in amazement. His mind stopped for a few seconds as it digested this information. The sniper's words were now corroborated. *I have something to go on, a real lead.*

"You may find this hard to believe, but today someone else told me the trail leads to Rome," Matt said.

"How? When?" Scott asked, as he showed wide-eyed amazement at hearing this.

Matt gave him the details of the sniper's revelation. He left out the method of extraction.

"What are we going to do?" Scott asked.

"All trails now lead to Rome. We're going to get the man behind this. I suggest you call our friend Monsignor McGregor and tell him we'll be there tomorrow."

"What should I tell him?"

"Tell him that we obtained information giving us a good reason to believe that someone connected to the Vatican murdered Bridget. We're coming to kill the bastard."

18

***

ROME, ITALY

THE IMPERIAL ROMAN SKY SPARKLED BLUE AS MATT AND SCOTT WALKED out of the Fiumicino Airport, where they took a taxi into the Eternal City to reach the Vatican. After showing their passports to the Swiss Guard at the side entrance, they were escorted to the office of the assistant to the Cardinal Secretary of State. Before their arrival, Monsignor Jonathan McGregor had requested they meet him in his office. Jonathan rose from his desk and came around to greet them when they entered.

"My condolences on the loss of Bridget. I pray for her soul every day," he said, his Scottish accent present in every sentence he uttered. He had a handsome face and still had a full head of sandy hair, and his steel-gray eyes saw everything, the trademark of a former spy. He indicated for them to take seats around a small conference table. "Would you like coffee?"

"Please," Scott responded. Matt wanted to get moving and not waste time drinking coffee. He wanted to tighten his hands on the culprit that contracted for Bridget's murder. *That's why they we're here.* But while they waited for the drinks to arrive, Matt took the opportunity to look around. The office provided a view of the Vatican gardens. The walls, a dull gray in color, held paintings of various saints, and a large crucifix hung behind Jonathan's desk. The wood-work around the windows displayed a high gloss shine.

"I've been doing some more investigation since Scott called me," Jonathan said. "The trail you are following seems to lead you to someone here at the Vatican. I've nothing concrete, but something has emerged that I believe may warrant your attention. I'm in no posi-tion to do it myself for reasons that pertain to my station here. I do want to help, though."

The coffee arrived, including one for Matt, and once the cups were filled and the server departed, Jonathan continued. "Captain Grossman, whom I believe you remember from our trip to Washing-ton, has provided me with some information that he believes is the singular link to any type of conspiracy here in Rome."

"He's the guy who helped you swindle—sorry, *acquire* the Bible of Constantine," Scott said as he did a mea culpa on his chest.

"The same," Jonathan said, "and he's the one who provided me the single shred of evidence that may lead you somewhere. The curator of the Vatican Museum, who would hear rumors about that sort of thing a long time before I would, couldn't help in this matter, even though he did attempt to find out about any rumors he heard."

"So, what have you got for us to go on?" Matt asked. They needed to find out the name, and then get moving. He wanted the man who'd put the hit on Bridget.

"There is a group, one I thought had gone dormant. However, it appears still to be active and extremely secretive. It is the remnants of the Agnus Dei society."

"Oh, no. Not those bastards," Scott blurted out.

"I take your point, Scott," Jonathan said. "They were the ones who almost got you and Bridget killed when you recovered the Crown of Thorns. I can understand your hatred of them. But remember, I was one of them, and I did save you both from certain death at the hands of that insane cardinal."

"True," Scott conceded.

"Well, there appears to be another cardinal, who has assumed the leadership mantle of the society. Cardinal Pedro Menendez, a member of an important curia of the church, has a residence here. The intelligence we gathered suggests he and some of his followers have expressed hatred against you Donavans for your role in humbling the Vatican into altering its position concerning the objects you discovered." McGregor stopped while he took a sip of his coffee.

"You may want to pay this cardinal a visit. I've not tried to contact him in order not to tip off anything you might plan. Would you like for Captain Grossman to accompany you? It might be prudent to take someone familiar with Rome and the Vatican with you. I briefed him on your mission here."

Matt rotated his head toward Scott with a questioning look. He wanted to know what he thought of the idea. Scott nodded his approval and then said, "Sounds like a plan. How do we get there?"

"I arranged for a special car for your use. It has all the modern electronics. Grossman will drive to keep what you are doing known only to the four of us."

"Great," Matt said. Finally, they would be taking action.

Jonathan went over to his desk and pushed a button on the console.

A few seconds later, a knock came on the door, and Captain Alfred Grossman, a commander in the Swiss Guard, entered. A strikingly handsome man with a military bearing, standing over six feet tall with blond hair and shining blue eyes. He wore a tailored blue blazer, tan pants, and a pale yellow open-collar shirt.

They shook hands since formal introductions were unnecessary, as Captain Grossman had interacted with them in the past.

"May I suggest we get going?" Matt said, but it was more than just a suggestion. He wanted to move, and now.

The drive through the crowded Roman streets took three quarters of an hour before they arrived at the address Grossman sought. The residence sat on the top of a rise in a luxurious sector of the city. The walls of the various villas fronting the road displayed guarded gates with security cameras visible to anyone who looked up.

Matt occasionally looked over at Scott, who didn't take his eyes off the laptop screen now that he had connected to the car's Wi-Fi.

Grossman hadn't spoken during the drive, and this had given Matt time to think. He'd failed to identify any strong motive for the Vatican to murder Bridget. Opportunity and means, yes, but motive appeared almost nonexistent. That remained to be seen, though, and this cardinal might provide that missing link.

Scott interrupted his thoughts. "I've localized the IP used to send the email. We're close. I'll have the address in a few minutes."

"You sure?"

"Just wait a second."

The car stopped in front of a gated entrance. "May I suggest that if the cardinal isn't at home, I present my credentials and we position ourselves to wait for his arrival?" Grossman said.

"Great. Let's do it," Matt said.

"I got the street address from where it looks like the emails originated," Scott announced. "It's Six Via del Peperino."

Matt looked at the plaque on the wall beside the entrance gate. It read 6 Via del Peperino.

19

───────

CARDINAL'S RESIDENCE

Captain Grossman presented his Vatican credentials to the guard at the entrance to the cardinal's residence, and the gates opened. He drove the short distance to the house, ending in a circular road in the anterior of the house. He stopped the car in front of the main entrance. Matt and Scott followed him up the steps to the entry door and waited while the Swiss Guard pulled on the cord to announce their presence. It took a full minute before a gray-haired lady in a maid's uniform came to the door.

"Good day," Grossman said in Italian. "We are looking for Cardinal Menendez." He showed her his Vatican credentials.

The maid looked a little put out, standing with her arms akimbo. She grimaced and shook her head. "Don't you know the cardinal is at an Agnus Dei meeting?" she responded in the local language.

Grossman translated for Matt and Scott.

"Ask her when he'll be back," Matt said.

The maid turned her face toward Matt. "That's all right. I understand English. You sound American," she said.

"I am. Could you help us in a matter of some urgency?" Matt asked.

"Please, excuse my manners. Come in." She led them into a large sitting room. "I can make some coffee for you if you would like? I'm sure the cardinal would want me to offer his hospitality to Americans. He has done so before."

"I'd love some," Scott said. "We've been up most of the night on a flight."

"Please be seated," she said after she led them into a waiting area. The room was decorated in a simple Roman style and also displayed a massive crucifix on the wall, with a picture of the Virgin Mary hanging beside the window. A table in the middle of the room held a single candle.

"So, he's not home now. Do you know when he'll return?" Matt asked.

Grossman looked at Matt, who huffed and paced around the room. He could tell that Matt was wound tight. The man had been rushing and pushing all of them ever since his arrival in Rome.

"In a little while, I believe. You know he's been away these past three weeks and only returned yesterday. I don't know exactly when he'll get home, but he would want me to offer you his hospitality," she said and left the room.

"I didn't know about this meeting the cardinal is attending. Like Jonathan said, we hadn't done anything to warrant raising any flags. Excuse me while I go outside to make a few calls to see about more information," Grossman offered.

He stood and left.

* * *

MATT NOTICED SCOTT SIGNALING HIM THAT HE WANTED TO TELL HIM something. He wondered if Scott had bungled something with his reliance on technology, and now needed to explain some error to him.

"What did you want?" he addressed Scott, who now approached.

Scott said, "I can't use the hot spot from my phone to run this latest program I received from my friend. I'll need a good Internet signal for it to load. We don't have one in this room. After I make a connection, it'll restart with the new patch to the software he sent, as there seems to be a previous internal defect it encountered and this should correct the problem."

"Get on with it," Matt said impatiently.

The maid returned, ushered them into a living room, and served the coffee. While she poured cups for them, she informed them, "My name is Maria. My daughter lives in America, in San Diego. She married a US Navy doctor. I love Americans. What can I do to help you?"

"We traced some computer usage to this address. Is it possible for us to see the owner's computer?"

"I think I found another problem." Scott didn't explain further, just put down his coffee and went back to the entrance hall. He placed his laptop on the windowsill nearest to the car. Matt followed him.

"The program is now restarting itself. This may take a few minutes. I needed to have a good connection with the Wi-Fi in the car, as it's much faster than my cell. There appears to be something wrong with my initial findings. The software is finding some sort of a flaw. This is the neatest program I've ever seen."

"What is it? Tell me now." Matt tried to hide the impatience he felt, but failed in his effort. "We don't have all day."

"Matt, you need to slow down. Let me do my work with this new program my hacker friend sent me for finding an IP address. It won't take long," Scott said. "You haven't slowed down since Bridget died. Take a breath, my friend. We're all here to help you."

Before he could continue, Grossman returned and said, "Matt, I agree with Scott. It might be a good idea to calm yourself, from what I've seen. You're wound too tight, as we say in the military. You won't be able to think straight if you stay at this intense level. Just an observation."

"I agree," Scott added. "This cardinal is a big deal. You can't just treat him like some gangster."

Matt heard them, but in his mind he kept going over what he wanted to do concerning this prelate. The man appeared somehow connected to Bridget's death. He would take whatever steps he needed to in order to acquire information about her. If it meant roughing up the priest, he would do it. He had to get the name of the person behind her murder. And if the cardinal turned out to be the guilty party, then he would do what he'd told Gerti. No questions asked.

Matt ignored their advice. They didn't get it. Even though Scott had lost his sister, he still had a wife and a future with a child on the way. Matt, on the other hand, had lost everything important in his life. Someone had killed his Bridget, taken his love and his life from him. Now he didn't care what he had to do or who he had to hurt to get the bastard—whatever it took, he would do it.

20

CARDINAL'S ARRIVAL

They heard a car entering the drive, then a door closed, and the car departed. Matt and his companions stood in a large drawing room when the cardinal arrived. The priest filled the door frame with his massive bulk, nearing sixty years old but with snow-white hair, cloaked in the red garb of a prince of the Roman Catholic Church. He entered without an entourage.

"Who are you? Why are you in my house?" he asked in passable but heavily accented English. Their dress probably gave them away, the shoes being the obvious giveaway. Many observers could pick out Americans by the style of footwear they wore.

Captain Grossman approached and presented his credentials.

"That doesn't answer my question. Why are you in my house, and who are these men?"

"I'm Matt Higgins, and this is Scott Donavan," Matt said as he approached the man without extending his hand.

At that moment, Grossman's phone rang. He looked at it and said, "I'll go outside to take this. It's important." He left.

"Are you the brother of Bridget Donavan?" the cardinal asked Scott, paying no attention to Grossman's departure.

"I see you know the name," Matt said. "We're here to ask you some questions."

"Make an appointment with my office if you want to have a meeting." The cardinal sneered at them. "I don't want to discuss anything with you, especially about that little…" He searched for a word but didn't seem to find it, his face turning red with rage. "About that little tart's fate," he finally managed. "She inflicted immense problems on our society, and now she is no longer able to."

Matt moved with blinding speed. He had lost the little patience he had tried to show. This man's arrogance and defamation of Bridget pissed him off. He slammed the cardinal into a chair behind where he stood. "I like the idea of having a meeting with you right now, and you better watch your mouth," he shouted, leaning down so he was nose to nose with the intimidated prelate.

The man's eyes went wide. "Where is that Swiss Guard? You are a maniac."

At this point, Matt sought information, and he would get it even if he had to kill this man. Rage inflamed his heart. The cardinal had unknowingly pushed the wrong button. Matt felt himself lose it. Now anger and hatred drove his actions.

"You're a cardinal, and I really don't want to kill you, but that all depends on your answers. Capisce?" Matt asked.

The cardinal nodded slowly.

Scott opened his laptop and moved out of the room. As he departed, he said over his shoulder, "My program is running now, with the latest patch from my friend. I should get a definite answer soon," he said. As an afterthought, he added, "Please hold off doing anything rash till I get my results."

"Cardinal Menendez," Matt said, never taking his eye off the man, ignoring Scott's entreaty, "I've obtained information that you hired someone to kill Bridget Donavan. The man gave up that detail with his dying breath. Our computer experts traced an email that links the killer to your computer here in Rome. So, you see why I think you're the killer." He slapped the man.

"I don't know what you're talking about. You're not making sense."

Matt reached down and grabbed the cardinal by the front of his cassock, pulled him to his feet, and breathed into his face. The man's eyes went wide, exhibiting real fear as Matt gripped him by the throat. He tried to pull Matt's hand away but lacked the strength to free himself from the viselike grip. Matt assumed that no one had ever attacked this cardinal in such a manner.

"Come on, quit playing dumb. You're the man who had reason to kill Bridget for what she did to your society. Your predecessor jumped from a helicopter and, with Bridget's help, Jonathan McGregor decimated your organization. I now believe you had definite motive. You have the money to contract someone to solve a problem you experienced with the Donavans." Matt kept squeezing the man's neck, lessening his stranglehold when he saw him signal with his hands that he wanted to talk.

"No. No, you aren't correct. Sure, we had reason to hate the Donavans, but after the events surrounding the return of the icon, we have no reason to feel any continued animosity toward them. I tell you, I don't know what you are talking about," the cardinal managed to say in halting English. He could, without doubt, feel Matt's hands applying more pressure to his neck.

Matt squeezed the man's neck until he saw the pallor of his skin change. The cardinal again wanted to say something, so he lessened the pressure slightly.

"I'm sorry for what I said about Ms. Donavan. We did not do what you are accusing us of. I swear it," the cardinal rasped out of his constricted throat.

Grossman reentered. "Let the cardinal go, Matt. Now."

"Wait," Scott shouted, running into the room behind Grossman. "He's telling the truth. He didn't do it."

Matt somehow managed to hear what Grossman shouted. He registered it. Scott's pronouncement made an entrance into his conscious mind. He released the chokehold inch by inch. As he reduced the pressure, the cardinal gasped and fell to the floor, clutching at his throat.

"What?" Matt shouted as he regained control of his emotions.

"What the hell are you talking about? We know this guy sent the emails." Matt felt his rage going ballistic. "What are you saying? We got all this wrong?" Matt screamed in an irate voice.

"He didn't do it," Scott said and repeated it again. He moved over to where Matt stood. "I discovered that he isn't the man in Rome, because there is no man here, but you were hell-bent on getting here and confronting him. The timeframes didn't add up. I tried to warn you to slow down. Now, I know where the emails originated. It's not Rome. Listen to me. It wasn't Rome."

"So you're wrong. What good is your program if it isn't accurate?" Matt shouted at Scott.

"Why don't you use your FBI assets? They have more capability than I have. Use them or get off my back."

"You know I can't. We're off-book now, and I'd be fired." He took a deep breath. "Sorry, I'm making bad decisions without thinking. I simply want to get to Bridget's killer."

Scott nodded understanding.

"Grossman, what did you find out?" Matt shouted.

While he waited for Grossman to reply, the maid returned. They all stood still and waited. She had escorted the cardinal to another room. She said, "The cardinal said I should call the police. I must do that now."

"Where's the cardinal's computer?" Scott asked. He moved to intercept her movement toward the phone.

"I'll take care of that call," Grossman said to Maria.

"The cardinal has a desktop computer here in his office, but I don't think he uses it. He is always on his laptop. Come. I'll show you," Maria said.

Scott and Matt followed her into a small room with a computer terminal mounted on a small desk with a small screen. "He has a young nephew who comes to visit, and the boy plays games on this computer since the cardinal never uses it."

Scott powered up the computer and found the IP address of the machine.

"It's the one the email came from on my original scan."

"When did this email come from here? I'm sure no one has used this for over three weeks," the maid said.

"Where was the cardinal the last three weeks?" Matt asked.

"He visited Brazil," she answered.

Grossman joined them again. "I called Jonathan and updated him," he said to Matt sub voce, then turned to the group and said, "When I went out of the room during your discussion with the cardinal, I also called the Vatican travel office to check on him. She's right. He and five priests spent the last three weeks in Brazil at an ecumenical conference of the Latin American churches."

"Three weeks?" Scott said. "This is definite proof the emails were planted on this machine to distract us."

"What? How?" Matt asked. He moved over to the computer and flopped down into a chair to examine it.

The sound of glass breaking reached his ears as he raised his eyes to the computer. The bullet missed his head by mere inches. He grabbed Scott, pulled him to the floor, then sprang up and tackled Maria as another bullet plowed into the wall above their heads.

Grossman ran outside on hearing the shots.

A few seconds went by before the sound of gunfire erupted somewhere beyond the window. Two shots. Then silence.

Grossman ran back into the room. "I shot and killed the shooter. He had started to flee, but turned and tried to fire at me. I fired first. Are you all right?" He looked at each in turn to search for wounds.

"I have to check on the cardinal," Maria said in a shaky voice and departed.

"Thank you," Matt said to Grossman. "What now?"

"The police will be involved, but I'll report that I think this attack appeared to be focused on the cardinal. They will defer to our police at the Vatican. It will be handled in a quiet manner. I need to go outside and do a few things. I'll be back in a minute." On his return he said, "I called the police and took photos of the shooter and his fingerprints on a piece of the glass from the shattered window. We should have his identity in no time."

Maria returned. "He is resting, but I think you should go before he comes down. He is rather upset, even angry. I have never seen him this distressed. Please go."

"How are you?" Matt asked. He felt sorry for the old lady, who appeared to be on the verge of shock with her ashen face.

He received a nod and a raised hand with a slight wave as a reply.

Matt smiled at her and then went over to Grossman. He whispered, "Do whatever you can to smooth this over."

"I think your friend McGregor will need to handle it. It'll take someone of his stature to placate this cardinal. He'll want something to remain silent, and that's Jonathan's bailiwick," Grossman whispered into Matt's ear as he moved toward the door.

When Scott looked up from his computer, his face had turned serious. "I think we should thank the lady and depart."

Captain Grossman said, "Excellent idea. We can talk in the car."

They thanked Maria for her offer to help. "I'm sorry for the mess in the house," Matt said. He could see her trembling. No wonder, but now she seemed to be regaining her composure.

"Think nothing of it." She stood up. "Now I have something to dine out on for a long time. I witnessed a shoot-out, like in the Wild West, no? That's so exciting."

"You're some lady. Again thanks, and the police will be here soon. I would appreciate you not mentioning that we were here, only Captain Grossman," Matt said.

She nodded.

Matt grabbed Scott by the arm and hurried him out of the house. He had almost killed the man. His actions were wrong in every aspect, so what the hell was he thinking? He had to get himself under control. If he didn't, he might inadvertently kill an innocent person next. He couldn't let that happen.

Now the cool night air hit him in the face and brought him back to earth. He wanted time to think. He decided they needed to depart immediately and use the flight time to regroup, because he realized he had to get some self-control and tone down the anger. He would not do Bridget any good by continuing to fly off the handle; he had to return to being a logical FBI agent. Grossman and Scott joined him in the car.

"What did you find out that you didn't want to say in there?" Matt asked.

As Grossman drove the car out the gate, he placed his cell to his ear.

Scott took a few seconds before answering. "My new patch on the previous software cut through all those false leads and traced the email back to the original source—an IP in St. Petersburg."

Grossman interrupted Scott. "I received information on our attacker. It seems he worked as a contract killer and is known to work for the highest bidder—a hit man open to any contract," Grossman said. "But lately he's been working for a Middle Eastern country, the Iranians, according to my sources."

"The Iranians!" Matt exclaimed. "That makes no sense."

Matt requested that Captain Grossman take them to the airport. He sent a text to the crew, telling them to prepare for an immediate departure. Matt felt his spirit sag. The adrenaline from the confrontation with the cardinal seeped out of his body. The trip had proven futile. They'd obtained nothing to go on but an IP address in Russia, another potential red herring.

"In my follow-up analysis with this program, it determined the emails appearing to be sent from the cardinal were backdated and were planted there a few days ago. Probably when his nephew played on the computer."

"What the hell does this mean?" Matt asked. "Couldn't you have found this out before we raced here?"

"No. It was due to that TOR. Remember I told you about it before. There are levels upon levels of deception built into a TOR. The name stands for 'the onion router.' So our program had to peel back layer after layer to get to the real IP source. It takes time, and there are always traps built in to prevent someone from cracking the code. So it demands a certain type of experience for a great hacker to break through the firewalls. The layers we experienced deposited false trails. We now know the cardinal took a trip to Brazil at the same time the emails were sent from his computer in Rome. Which is impossible for him to do, but they appeared to originate from his house in order to be flagged as authentic. I've now determined that they weren't sent from the cardinal's computer, but made to look like it by some TOR." Scott held up his hand as he looked at the screen of his laptop.

"So, put it in English," Matt demanded.

"It appears the TOR sent us on a wild goose chase," Scott continued. "This new patch to my program has verified the original location of the emails was accurate. Someone noticed we were tracking the email and employed an onion router to deceive us. Like two or three days ago. I can now tell you with absolute certainty they originated in Russia, St. Petersburg to be precise. Now I'm also getting a text message in DOS format from the program that's flagging another problem it discovered. Some malware placed on my phone."

"What now?" Matt queried.

"My phone has been cloned."

"What do you mean?" Matt almost shouted. "How could that happen?"

"It means that someone's been listening to all of our conversations."

"When did that happen?" Matt queried as he glared at Scott.

"No idea. It could've been anytime. The program picked it up after I connected the computer to the hot spot on my phone. But, logically it must've been in the recent past. Like, after all this started. Hell, it could have happened at the funeral, in the hospital in New York, or in Washington, at an airport, almost anywhere."

"I can't believe this shit is happening. You couldn't have discovered this earlier?" Matt indicated, gesturing for Scott to give him the phone. "Captain, could you to pull over on this bridge and stop?"

Grossman did as requested.

Matt exited the car with Scott's phone in hand. He opened the cell, removed the battery, and ejected the SIM card. He snapped the SIM in half and threw the entire collection of parts into the river. He returned to the car and signaled for the driver to go on.

"Sorry, I had no way of knowing earlier. What now?" Scott asked.

"I want you to verify everything you told us again. Make sure this time that our information is accurate and not another false trail. We're going back to visit your father-in-law ASAP. We'll need his assistance for what I'm planning."

"What plan?"

"Wait and see."

21

ROBOCOP VOICE

"You're a bumbling fool," the synthetically altered voice shouted into the phone. "They found out the emails came from St. Petersburg. It won't take them long to figure out who you are and come after you. You need to handle the contract immediately."

"How do you know this?" the man asked, sweeping his long hair out of his face.

"I have ears on them. They will come after you. You haven't fulfilled your contract, and I will not complete the transfer of money to your account."

"I will complete the contract, and you will pay me the money. Give me some time."

The phone went dead in the man's ear. The caller had again underestimated him. With this information received, he would be prepared to handle the arrival of the targets. He'd failed to eliminate them in the States, but he would now handle it on his own turf. He wouldn't rely on unknown and untested outside help. He would use his own assets.

He picked the phone up and dialed a number. He didn't relish making this call, but he felt he had no choice. He had previously provided this group with weapons, and now he needed them to make the down payment on the order they'd submitted yesterday. But he needed them to pay him in men instead of money. They would be his army when the Americans arrived.

The Iranians would arrive within forty-eight hours. No Russian would be anywhere near the scene if anything went wrong. No blame could come his way to disrupt the delicate balance he maintained with the local cops. He and his men would be in Moscow when some terrorists attacked his home for some unknown reason. The police would attempt to solve the mystery of whatever happened at his house as he remained in Moscow and only two security guards remained behind to protect his estate.

Stupid Robocop. The man would be dealt with after he received his money for completing the contract. He had discovered where the man lived. Silencing the bastard would be a real pleasure, and he intended to make it permanent. The man treated him like an idiot with the theatrics of his call, but Dmitri had outmaneuvered the caller and knew to whom the voice belonged. Nobody outsmarted Dmitri Alexander Alexandrovitch.

* * *

MATT AND SCOTT ARRIVED ON SCHULTZ'S PLANE IN NEW YORK exhausted from the many hours of flying to and from Rome in such a short time. They went straight to Schultz's apartment on Central Park. As they exited the taxi, the sun made its last effort to illuminate the Manhattan skyline as it sank into the western horizon.

"Welcome," Schultz said on opening the door. "You both look like you could use a drink. I'm having my evening Dalmore scotch. Would you care to join me?"

"I'd like a double," Matt said. Scott nodded agreement.

They accepted the drinks from Schultz and took comfortable chairs in the sitting room.

"What did you learn?" Schultz asked.

Matt brought him up to date on the visit to Rome and the dead end they'd encountered at the cardinal's house.

"We did have a problem," Scott interrupted. "Someone was listening to what we did."

"How?" Schultz asked.

"My phone got cloned recently. They would know all that we were doing. Everything—where we went, and what we found out up till our departure from Rome."

"So whoever listened knows whatever you did and what you might do?" Schultz queried.

"Unfortunately, yes," Matt said. "Now we need to plan our next move."

"I think that's obvious," Scott said.

"What do you mean?" Schultz asked.

"Matt didn't mention that I've traced the email to its real source with the new upgrade I received. The original contract came from Russia."

Schultz refilled their glasses. "What are you thinking of doing?"

"Scott has worked on narrowing down the location. You know there's only one person there who has any connection to us. Scott told me about the trip that he and Bridget took to St. Petersburg, and that's where his software tells him the email originated. Bridget and Scott had some help from one of your colleagues there. I plan on going to visit that man and getting him to help."

Schultz sat down. He looked at Matt, then with deliberate intonation, asked, "You mean the uncle of the man one of you killed in Savannah?"

"Yes, Dmitri Alexander Alexandrovitch," Matt answered.

22

NEW YORK CONFERENCE

MATT TOOK A DRINK FROM HIS SCOTCH BEFORE SPEAKING AGAIN. SCOTT glanced at him in anticipation of hearing a plan. Schultz took a seat opposite them on a couch and also waited. An initial strategy had germinated in Matt's mind, but now, after the phone cloning, the security problem seemed much bigger than before. Someone had actually tracked their movements and might know where they would go next in their pursuit of the ultimate target.

"The fewer people who are aware of what we're planning, the better," Matt said. "We can't afford a leak of any kind. We're going after a killer. Make no mistake about it. Dmitri will kill us if we don't get him first. The man is smart and well connected. He'll use every asset at his command to neutralize us once he realizes we're coming after him."

"From what we learned about him during your last encounter with the Russians in Savannah, he could without doubt carry a grudge against you for being involved in the killing of his nephew," Schultz said.

"That provides the element of this puzzle that was absent in Rome," Matt said. "I can see this Dmitri has real motive. He controls the means, and he can create the opportunity by hiring killers."

"Are we going to Russia?" Scott asked.

"I have to. We can't expect him to come here, since he has no reason to do that," Matt said. He stood and walked over to the sliding glass door leading to the balcony overlooking Central Park. He looked out for a few seconds before rotating to face them.

"Matt, I'm not so sure that's the best course of action. Why not lure him to the US?" Schultz asked. "There must be some way to make that happen."

"We currently have no leverage over him. He's in his safe haven with no reason to come out. Do you have any ideas about what we could use to compel him to leave Russia?" Matt asked.

"Actually, no," Schultz said. "But could this be another red herring? You went to Rome on a false lead."

"I know, but this seems like the right course to me. We now identified a man who has motive." Matt took a sip of his drink.

"While you two were gone, I was thinking about how clever it was for my men to capture the shooter in Washington—but maybe it was too easy. Perhaps the organizer of all this planned for him to get caught and give us the Rome connection. It could have been set up before, and a mastermind criminal could think like that. Setting up all the pieces in advance for various contingencies."

"Good point," Matt said.

"Matt, perhaps we should take some time to evaluate all this. Is it wise to go rushing off to Russia? Mr. Schultz has a valid point. Look what happened the last time. We ran in like bulls in a china shop and damaged ourselves. This could be another set-up like he just points out," Scott said.

"Scott makes a good argument too," Schultz said.

"But Dmitri is the only lead. I say we go after him," Matt said. "Besides, I don't think he knows who shot his nephew. That info has never been released."

"Who did kill him?" Schultz said.

"Not important now," Matt replied.

Scott moved over to face Matt. "If you're going, I'm coming with you," he said. "I can continue to work on refining the location. I don't want us to get blindsided like we did in Rome. If for some unknown reason the email's physical position proves to be another false lead, I'll need to be there with you. You know, in case something changes due to the software I'm using."

"We'll need some funding and again the use of your plane, if possible." Matt looked at Schultz.

"I wish I could. Funding is no problem, but there is a problem with what you ask. I have to apply for clearance to enter Russian Federation airspace seven days in advance. Do you want to wait?"

"No," Matt said. "We'll go commercial. They fly every day and we both are fortunate enough to be able to get Russian visas before we go. So it'll be two days before we can leave, but that's better than seven."

"I want this man stopped before he can get at my daughter." Schultz hesitated a moment, then continued, "I mean, stopped before he gets to any of you."

"We're going to St. Petersburg. It may take some time to get at him, but at least we'll be in the belly of the beast, so to speak," Matt said.

"I'm a patient man, but if I feel it's taking too long, then I may be obliged to act," Schultz said.

"What do you mean by that?" Matt asked.

"Nothing. Really, nothing." Schultz took another drink from his glass and looked away from Matt.

Matt returned to the center of the room and signaled Scott it was time to depart by inclining his head toward the door.

Outside the apartment, Matt said to Scott, "I didn't like that last threat."

"It sort of took me by surprise. What do you think he would do if we can't get Dmitri?" Scott queried.

"I don't know. We better go to St. Petersburg and solve this matter so we never have to find out."

23

PLANNING THE TRIP

Gerti rose from her bed when she heard Scott call her name as he entered the house. Her heart beat faster in anticipation of seeing him. The fainting spells of the last few days were now waning, and she'd begun to feel like her old self. She saw him in the doorway to her room and gave him a warm and welcoming smile.

She reached him and they embraced. "It's so good to see you." She paused and then continued, "I love you so much, and I miss the hell out of you. You've been gone a long time, so could you please take your horny wife to bed?" she said with a coquettish smile. Scott hugged and kissed her passionately. Then he led her back to the bed and assisted her in getting comfortable.

Later she asked, "Tell me what's been happening."

"First of all, how are you really feeling?" he asked.

"A lot better after that, but being trapped here makes me feel like the acorn a squirrel put away for the winter. It's so isolated. Yes, I know it's necessary, but I want us to be together. We should be, since we just got married. Right?"

"I agree, and I've missed you. I'd rather have you here and alive than out there and—"

"I know. Give me a hug."

He took her in his arms and held her. After a minute, he took a seat on the side of the bed and they sat together. In vivid detail, he explained what had transpired in Rome and told her about the subsequent meeting with her father.

"So what now?" Gerti asked.

"We're going to St. Petersburg in the morning. I want to go to make sure we don't experience any screw-ups in the search for the final location of the IP address of the emails. I think it necessary for me to go with Matt. He's acted like a loose cannon on occasion, and I think I'd better go with him."

She looked at him for a long time. Her mind raced as she tried to figure out some way she could help him. Being confined to this safe house imposed severe limits on her movements, but not on her mental capabilities. Her thought processes, honed by years of observing her father and his methodology, kicked in.

"I have an idea. I can help with this trip to Russia. I'll call Val. You remember him. He saved our bacon the last time we were there. He knows me, and he'll be glad to help. He believes I'll take over for Father one day." She reached for her cell.

"Hang on," Scott said. "Let's talk about this. I thought we weren't going down that road, the one where you take over the company. We talked about raising our children away from the type of business your dad is in."

"You're right. I already explained to you what I intend to do for our future. What I have to do now is all in order to make that possible. I want what we planned more than anything now that the baby is on the way. You're going to Russia. I think you'll need some help, and I can get it."

"Why?" Scott asked.

"I'll arrange for someone to assist you over there. There's no other choice. If I don't, you'll be walking around blind in a place you know nothing about. Am I right?"

He conceded the point with a nod. "I guess I have to learn that you're the boss in many areas. We'll only be away for a few days, I hope. Promise me you'll stay here, no sneaking out or anything. I don't want to worry about your safety while I'm gone."

Without another word, she placed the call to Val. After a short conversation, in which she asked him to help Scott and Matt when they arrived in his country for a visit, she hung up. "He'll be waiting for you on arrival." She gave him Val's phone number.

"Now that we've settled that..." She pulled him down on top of her.

24

MATT ARRIVES IN ST. PETERSBURG

MATT AND SCOTT ARRIVED AT THE ST. PETERSBURG AIRPORT AT NOON. The temperature required a coat and gloves. The clear blue sky domed the capitol city without even a puff of a cloud.

Matt recalled that Scott and Gerti had visited here in their attempt to learn about the man behind the arms shipments to the United States. The FBI suspected Russians were delivering the weapons to homegrown terrorist groups. It proved to be a fact. During Scott and Bridget's visit to Russia, they'd learned the name Dmitri Alexandrovitch, compliments of a man named Val and his team.

After clearing Russian customs and immigration, they started walking toward a taxi stand. A muscular man over six feet tall with a full black beard approached them and held out his hand to Scott. "Welcome to Russia, Scott," the man said in English, with a slight British accent.

"Val, how did you know we'd be on this flight? I didn't plan on calling you until after we'd checked in to the hotel. This is Matt Higgins, by the way."

Val and Matt shook hands. He extended a warm welcome to Matt.

"How did you know we'd be on this plane?" Matt repeated Scott's query.

"Gerti told me you would be arriving today. We have our ways. If I couldn't find out what flight you were on after the call from Ms. Gerti, I wouldn't be of much use to you, now would I?"

"You maintain your methods. Do you know why we're here?" Scott asked.

"Not exactly. I would imagine it has something to do with Dmitri Alexandrovitch. Am I correct?"

"You got it," Matt said. "We'll be attempting to verify that he's the man responsible for trying to murder the four of us. You know that we killed his nephew in Savannah."

"Forgive me, Scott, I'm sorry about your sister," Val said without acknowledging Matt's comment. "I'll always remember her. Such a dynamic character and full of courage."

Matt looked away and tried not to show the welling emotion Val's mini eulogy conjured. The wound stayed open and sore. He had come here to deliver justice to the man he now believed had ordered her death. Nothing would deter him, and his goal remained crystal clear in his mind.

"Our friend Dmitri recently moved to a new location. His new house is a fortress. I suggest we take a ride to see it during the daylight."

"Is it heavily guarded?" Matt asked.

"From what we have been able to put together, it usually is. Today, however, the guards were reduced to two, and all the others have gone with Dmitri. We believe to Moscow, but I haven't confirmed his destination. The villa appears to be basically deserted." Val led them to a car. A driver grabbed their small suitcases and put them in the trunk.

"How far is it?" Scott asked.

"About a half hour or so. Just to let you know, we've been doing surveillance on it for some time for our own purposes."

On reaching the area of the city containing the villa, Matt noticed a large hill to the east side of it and walls surrounding three sides, with two of them dead-ending into a steep cliff. They observed the place from an elevated vantage point about half a mile away. There existed an extensive array of antennas over the roof on the second story of the house. The house stood back from the road about fifty meters and had a double door entrance gate.

"I believe this is the spot where the emails originated. But I can't understand why they'd leave the computers on if no one is here," Scott said.

"We need to get in there," Matt said.

"I suggest you go to your hotel and rest until this evening. I'll pick you up at eleven. Is that a good time?"

"Sounds like a plan," Matt said. He knew this would be the best course of action. Going in during daylight hours would be foolish even if the house remained unguarded. He'd love to go now, but reason dictated otherwise. He told himself that he'd gone off half-cocked too many times in the recent past. He wished he could call Liz and get overhead coverage of the place, but the fact that he was off-book doing his own thing prevented that. She would have a convulsion if she knew he was calling from Russia.

Liz would ask too many questions he didn't want to answer. She would undoubtedly query, "What the hell are you doing? You need to get back on the reservation. You are our asset and we want you to be in communication with us at all times." That would never work if he wanted to accomplish his mission. Besides, he sensed that Liz had a small crush on him, and he didn't want to hurt her in any way.

The director would rant with justifiable rage if he knew Matt had gone to Russia in his pursuit. He would order him home to prevent a possible diplomatic incident. In the end, he determined it would be better to do this his way and not the FBI's.

"These are for you," Val said as he handed each a Glock 9mm handgun and a pair of NVGs. "I'll have my men do surveillance of the house while we wait. We've found another good position a kilometer from here where we can see down into the property."

Matt's cell rang. He saw Liz's number and ignored the call. If he answered, she might tell him something he didn't want to hear. She was undoubtedly tracking his phone and probably knew his location.

"I'm giving you the latest pictures and diagrams we were able to acquire of the house. They're only a few hours old." Val handed them to Matt.

"Damn, I hoped to pay him a visit now," Matt sighed. He then looked at Val. "But we'll drop in on him tonight."

Val nodded.

25

BREAKING AND ENTERING

MATT ENJOYED A TWO-HOUR NAP IN HIS HOTEL ROOM BEFORE HIS CELL phone rang. On seeing the number belonged to Liz, he decided to ignore it again. Instead, he texted a short note that he would call her tomorrow. Anything to keep her at bay until he could complete his mission.

A knock at the door caused him to look at his watch. Val wasn't scheduled to arrive for another half hour. He presumed it would be Scott, but on opening his door, he found Val standing there.

"Come in. What's up?"

"I propose a slight change of plans," Val said. He took a seat in an armchair while Matt sat on the bed. "We've been observing the house for the last few hours and noticed another group repeatedly going by. One of that band stayed behind to conduct surveillance on the house. Lucky we're located further away and were able to observe all this without getting spotted. I don't know who they are, but I don't believe they're from Russia. Based on what I saw through my binos, I would guess Middle Eastern, probably Syrian, maybe Iranian or even Hezbollah personnel. Why they are here, I can't figure out. What's even more puzzling is why they are watching Alexandrovitch's house."

"How many are there?" Matt asked.

"Ten that we counted."

"Almost like a strike team," Matt said. He paused before continuing. "Perhaps they're there to do something against Dmitri. He may have shorted them in some arms transaction. Maybe that's why he's away. He might suspect they would come after him."

"I suppose that's possible, but why stake out a deserted house? It would be easy to see when Dmitri returned by the number of guards. Pass by once a day to determine that, not keep the house under constant surveillance. No one is currently there but the two watchers, and one of them is generally asleep after ten at night and the other dozes off in a chair at the entrance."

"Will either the guards or the people you observed interfere with our planned mission to visit the house?"

"I don't think so. We're going in through an unguarded entrance, a servant's gateway, actually. I called on a few friends to reinforce my men at the observation post. We'll have about fifteen or so who I'll position around the exterior of the house, and they will move to cover the house when we go in. They'll provide outside firepower in case anyone shows up unexpectedly," Val said.

"Sounds good. Let's pick up Scott on the way."

In the car, Matt told Scott that he would not be going in with him, as he needed someone on the outside as a precaution.

"I didn't come all this way to sit on my ass," Scott said. He looked angry at this new development.

"I know, but I think it would be the best course of action. We don't want to have all three of us in the house together. I need a lookout and some eyes on my back."

Scott nodded his understanding. He handed over a flash drive to Matt. "You'll need to insert this into the computer in the house to make certain that the email originated from that IP address. It'll give me some other information as well."

They stopped at a location two blocks south of the main entrance to Dmitri's house. In the darkness, the faint light of the streetlight at the corner illuminated the fire hydrant directly beneath it. The wind sent a chill through Matt. He zipped up his parka to the neck.

"Scott, I want you to stay here in the car. We'll use our private two-way comms and we'll be in constant touch. If anything happens, you'll have all the info I do and you can get away to safety with it. Understand?"

"I'd still like to go with you," Scott said, but Matt fixed him with a hard stare showing he would not brook any backtalk.

"Okay," Scott conceded.

"I'll lead," Val told Matt. "We're going to go around to the left side and through a garden entrance. It's never guarded at night. There are no lights on in the building, so we'll need the NVGs."

Matt put his around his neck at the same time Val did. They headed off. Matt gave Scott a farewell wave and a thumbs-up.

Getting in through the wall's side portal proved as easy as Val had suggested after he produced a key he'd somehow acquired that unlocked the gate. They entered the grounds. With the aid of the NVGs, they hurried across the open space, moving around two statues placed on the lawn, which would have remained unseen without the NVGs' help. They reached the servants' entrance to the house in short order. Val turned the knob and it opened. Matt realized there would be no need to keep the doors to the house locked with all the security Dmitri employed.

Val swung the door open. A rifle butt swished by his head, but he instantly ducked down and reacted automatically by attacking the man. He slammed his fist into the man's face and then aimed his knee toward his groin with a vicious upward thrust. The weapon flew from the guard's hands when Val made contact. Val regained his upright posture and, with the practiced movements of an expert, plunged a knife into the man's throat while covering his mouth to prevent any sounds from escaping.

"I thought you told me he slept after ten," Matt whispered to Val.

"Maybe we caught him on a pee break. Come on, we're alive, aren't we? Let's move," Val said and slapped Matt on the back.

"We need to ensure we don't make any more noise before we get out of here. Maybe we can leave without anyone knowing we've been here."

On searching the first-floor main entryway, Matt found nothing, but the design appeared to be a receiving and party area. He peeked out the glass panel in the front door. There he observed the guard with his head slumped over, sleeping. They climbed the palatial marble staircase to the second floor. There they opened and closed the doors on the first two rooms on the right and discovered they were small bedrooms. They entered the third room on the right side of the hall. Matt realized by the furniture that this had to be the office.

Val went over to the window. His phone buzzed a soft tone. He answered, and after listening for a couple of seconds, he looked at Matt. "There is a group of men heading this way. They came from the same vehicle we observed earlier. I believe they are coming here. The spotter they left behind surely saw us enter the house. We need to hurry. There's more of them than we thought, maybe twenty."

"Any good news?" Matt asked. He searched the large mahogany desk but found nothing of significance. On top of the desk, however, was a picture of a young girl with two elderly ladies. This might be important. Another single photo resided on Dmitri's desk; Matt intended to grab it later but then changed his mind, deciding that now was as good a time as any. With the two photos stashed away, he got back on with his search for the computer.

Val spoke into his phone. "Move our men into position. Be ready for action in two minutes."

"Do we have any time?" Matt asked.

Val moved over to where Matt had placed the pictures in his backpack. "They may be here before my men get set. They are moving quicker than I expected. I think we must go. Now."

Matt was now becoming desperate in his search for a computer. There must be one. This whole venture relied on finding the instrument that had transmitted the email and thereby verifying the culprit was indeed Dmitri.

Two beautiful paintings hung behind the desk. Matt snapped a photo of them and then lifted each to see if a panel or safe was buried there behind them. No luck, so he continued around the room without finding anything useful. He took a few snapshots of the room. He needed to find the damn computer, but where?

At that moment, Matt heard Scott's voice come over his earpiece, but before he could acknowledge it, the sound of automatic gunfire erupted at the front of the house, where bullets smashed through windows on the ground floor.

"We gotta go," shouted Val.

"Not yet," Matt responded. He started to grab everything he could and throw it into his backpack. At least he could make it look like a robbery. He snatched other pictures, the papers from the desk, and then, before he could capture anything else, he heard a sound from the hall.

In the next second, a man holding an AK appeared in the door and rounds peppered the room. Matt and Val dove for the floor.

Val let out a scream.

26

ESCAPE

The attacker continued to fire in all directions without concentrating on any one spot in the room; since he didn't wear NVGs, he didn't realize the targets had already dived for cover. Matt heard and felt the rounds pass over his head as they scampered in a low crawl toward the far wall. He pulled his Glock from its belt holster with one rapid and fluid movement, then sprang up and fired two bullets into the man standing in the doorway shining green in his NVGs.

Matt rushed to Val. "You all right?" he asked as Val rose up, grasping his shoulder.

"Yeah, the bastard nicked me on the shoulder. Thanks. Now we need to go."

Matt took off his NVGs and turned on the overhead light. No use in pretending not to be here. Someone knew they had penetrated the house and was intent on eliminating them. He still needed to find Dmitri's computer. Once the room became illuminated, he noticed a single door on the side wall, flanked by two huge bookshelves. He flung the door open and stepped into what he believed to be the owner's bedroom. A large four-poster bed dominated the center of the room, with two wide television monitors hung on the wall for viewing from the bed. After he turned on the light, he scanned the area in quick, short movements. A desktop computer rested on a small stand near the bed.

"I found the computer," he shouted to Val. It took a second to insert the flash drive and power up the machine. Multiple weapons being fired outside of the house rattled the peace of the night. He wanted to have this drive inserted and connected to Scott's machine in case they didn't make it out. The computer would weigh too much to attempt to extract it with them. He didn't want to think of not making it out, but that loomed as a possibility with the current assault on their position.

Val grabbed him by the arm and tried to force Matt to follow him out.

At that moment his earpiece erupted.

* * *

"ALL HELL IS BREAKING LOSE OUT HERE," SCOTT SAID FOR MATT TO hear over his earpiece. "Val's men are trying to keep them in a kill zone in front of the house, but some got in. Watch yourself. I'm still up here on the hill away from the house."

He looked down from his vantage point overlooking Alexandrovitch's estate. He could see tracer rounds impacting the outside of the house, their brilliant red trails lighting up the night. As he observed the firing concentrated on the house, he picked up movement closer to his location. Bullets started to impact nearby. Scott yelled at the men around him. They were also under attack. His lack of Russian delayed their comprehension of the warning, but his loud shouting and pointing alerted his guard detail to the danger. In seconds, they returned fire and one of them grabbed Scott. They ushered him down the backside of the observation hill.

They reached the location where he had left Matt and Val. The guards stooped and took up firing positions aiming in the direction from which they had come. His companion did the same thing on the opposite side of the street.

Scott quickly collected himself despite the pounding of his heart and decided to contact Matt with an update.

"We're back where we split up. The attackers found the OP and attacked us. I think we're safe now. Hurry up so we can get out of here."

"I'm at the computer. Inserted the flash drive," he heard Matt say in a stressed voice.

Scott opened his laptop and acquired the signal from the device attached to Dmitri's computer. He waited to see if he could receive any information from the drive. Then a large amount of data started to arrive.

"I'm getting info," he informed Matt. "Go, and leave the flash. It's gonna take a while longer to get all the data on the drive."

"No can do. Nothing that can be traced back to us. How much more time?"

"I'll get the document files and emails and won't bother with anything else. Maybe one or two minutes."

* * *

"That's all I needed," Scott said in Matt's earpiece. "It's definitely the computer that originated the emails. Now bug out of there. These guys out here are shooting everyone. Val's men are attempting to eliminate the attackers and starting to succeed. They killed the ones that attacked me and are now moving to eliminate those at the house."

Matt heard the urgency in Scott's voice. He realized that they could be trapped inside by the superior force that now stormed the house. Time to go. He let Val pull him away from the computer as he jerked out the flash drive, which had somehow transmitted all the required information to Scott. One day, he would learn more about this tech stuff—if he got out of here alive, that was.

"Follow me. We have to go. They'll be covering the front and side entrances. I know a different way out. We need to get downstairs first." They exited the bedroom into the hallway, leaving the light on and the door open.

They ran toward the stairway and found two men with automatic weapons stood at the bottom of the stairs with their AKs raised. They opened fire. Matt tugged Val back as the bullets slammed into the ceiling. The next second, Val pushed Matt toward a door two down on the right side. Both men kept their weapons out and ready. They entered the room and shut the door.

"I think they'll go for the lighted doorway on down the hall. Get ready," Val said.

The sound of footsteps running up the stairway reached Matt's ears. Val signaled for him to stay still. The men ran past the door. As they did, Val jerked open the door and both men stepped into the hall. They fired multiple rounds into their attackers' backs and sent them tumbling forward.

Matt rushed over and looked down at one of the dead. The light from the bedroom illuminated his features.

"My bet, he's Iranian," Matt said. In his mind they were the most likely culprits to be associated with Dmitri.

Val searched the other man and found a wallet. "Follow me," he said.

At the end of the hall, Val opened a door into a large room. He crossed it and sent three rounds into the floor-to-ceiling solid-case window, shattering the glass. Matt saw why he had blown out the window. A fire escape ladder hung outside.

"Didn't want to waste time getting it to open," Val said with a smile. "With all the gunfire out front, no one will notice a few rounds going off in here. We need to hurry and head for that wall over there." He pointed to where he wanted Matt to go. Matt saw his objective. It comprised an integral part of the perimeter defense of the house by extending into the side of a cliff. "You go first, I'll cover you going down."

Matt scaled the ladder and moved away from the house. He stopped short of the wall some sixty feet from the house and took up a firing position to cover Val's descent. Without warning, a man appeared with an AK in the window over Val's head. He looked down and saw Val climbing down the rungs as quickly as he could. Before the attacker could raise his weapon, Matt opened fire and watched as the man fell out the window. At this distance, and firing from a stance, he didn't want to take the risk of not neutralizing his target, so he'd used his entire magazine. The falling man and Val hit the ground at the same time.

Matt slipped the empty magazine out and reloaded as Val came running to his position. They both climbed over the wall and ran a block before Val raised his hand.

"Let's stop here. I'll call my men for a sitrep."

"Scott, can you hear me?" Matt asked. He didn't receive any answer.

After a short conversation, Val said, "Scott is fine. My men evacuated him. He's most likely out of comm range for your earpiece from our location. They tell me they cleared the house of the attackers. They eliminated all the ones who arrived in the van." He gleamed with pride at this statement.

"Let's take a look at that wallet you lifted," Matt said.

"There is a passport inside. It's Iranian." Val handed it to Matt, confirming Matt's suspicion.

"They knew we were going to be here. How did they know? They were after us, not Dmitri. He's not here, and they knew that," Matt said. "We have to get out of Russia. They'll come after us again if we stay here."

"You are right, my friend. Now we hurry and get away from here. I can hear the police sirens."

"We know that Dmitri sent the email putting a contract on us. Now we need to plan how to get him. Since he's not here, and you don't know where he is or when he'll return, we can't afford to stay in Russia. We have to go home and plan our next moves based on what we've learned." Matt slapped Val on the back. "Really appreciate what you did."

Matt returned to their hotel and found Scott in his room.

"What a night. Val's men decided to evacuate me from the area and brought me here for my safety," Scott said, looking up. "Great work on getting at the computer. You're not going to believe what I discovered."

"What?" Matt demanded.

"The emails putting the hit on us certainly originated from that computer. No question of that now. There is one other thing that I located. I found a Word document that Dmitri probably copied from some or all of an email. I didn't extract the actual email, but I don't think you'll miss the significance."

Scott went over to his computer and hit a few keys. He returned with the laptop and turned it for Matt to see the message he had found in the document.

Kill Bridget Donavan, Scott Donavan and Matt Higgins. No collateral damage.

27

MATT PLANS TO USE KARIM

Matt raised the glass of scotch his host had given him. They clinked glasses. "What did you learn in Russia?" Schultz asked. They were seated in Schultz's apartment in New York overlooking Central Park. Matt took a few moments to enjoy the warm feeling of the beverage and then opened his backpack to display the photos he'd taken of the office space and the framed pictures taken from Dmitri's desk.

"I examined them on the plane ride here," Matt said. "But I have to admit, I can't find anything useful. The most beneficial thing we retrieved came from the computer hack that Scott did on the desktop computer using his software. He confirmed that the order to kill us originated from that machine. You'll be glad to hear that your daughter's name isn't on the list. The problem in all this is that we have to get to Dmitri to find out who hired him."

"You have no idea who that could be?" Schultz asked.

"Absolutely none, at this time," Matt responded. "I'm formulating a plan to use Karim, who might still maintain contact with our favorite Russian crime lord."

"What are you planning?"

"We talked before about some way to get at Dmitri, but we have no leverage. Maybe I can employ this Karim to cajole him into coming out. Dmitri seems to have disappeared, maybe gone into hiding, and I plan on getting him to come out to visit us."

"How?" Schultz asked.

"Right this minute, I'm not sure, but I'm working on it."

* * *

MATT HELD THE PHONE AWAY FROM HIS EAR AS HE WAITED FOR IT TO BE answered.

"Where the hell have you been?" Liz almost shouted into the receiver.

"I took a little trip, but it didn't work out." He took a breath and waited for some pithy comment from Liz, but none came, so he continued, "Remember the director gave me approval for a plan I had to use Karim?"

"Yes. What's your plan?" came syllable by syllable in the enunciated response.

"I implore you to get his release order processed."

"Are you out of your mind? He hasn't given up the intel we want."

"Be that as it may, the director told me to find the bastard who killed Bridget and attempted to kill me. I need this scumbag to help me capture him. Make it happen."

"He wants to see you," came her answer.

Matt hung up and headed for the safe house in the Virginia countryside. The director could wait until his plan coalesced and he could talk coherently about it. The plan hadn't really completely come together in his mind, but by the time he arrived, he believed he would have worked out the details.

An hour later, Matt sat down opposite Karim. The man appeared somewhat surprised by his visit and didn't say anything. Matt waited before speaking. He knew Karim to be curious, and undoubtedly the man was already formulating lies to take advantage of anything he said.

"I may have a job for you. It'll get you out of here for a while, and possibly forever, depending on how well you do."

Karim stared at him, in obvious disbelief by the expression on his face. He looked Matt in the eye and said, "What do you want?"

"It's simple. I want you to set up a delivery of arms from the Russian who supplied your man in Savannah. We'll fund whatever you need to establish yourself with an import-export office to be used as a transfer point to the people you will sell to."

Karim started to glow, and a big smile spread across his face.

"I'm the only person you will sell anything to," Matt said.

The smile disappeared. "I don't maintain contact with that man."

"You're lying. You're just maneuvering to try to get more out of me. That's the deal. Take it or start thinking of how much you'll enjoy the sunshine in Gitmo."

"Since you put it that way, what are the details?"

Matt filled him in on what he wanted Karim to accomplish. Karim would have to contact all the people he knew in the illegal arms trade and spread the word that he had opened a new business. Karim needed clients and would provide any materials ordered. His most important task remained getting information on Dmitri Alexandrovitch. All the responses he received, whether by Internet or in person, would be monitored.

Before Matt left, he looked at Karim in as stern a manner as he could muster. "If you fail me, you know what will happen. If you try to run, I swear to you now, I'll kill you. If you accomplish this and I get Bridget's murderer, I'll do everything possible to secure your release."

Karim nodded his acceptance.

"Be prepared to leave here soon and start your new life as an arms dealer. Try anything stupid and I'll put you down."

28

SOTHEBY'S BACKUP PLAN

When Matt left Karim's location, he felt elated about the future. He now could put into motion his embryonic plan to attract Dmitri to come to the States, as he couldn't go back to Russia. It might take a little while, but now he had his target and a time. He would proceed with deliberation and detailed planning to exact his final vengeance. The first step would be to get Scott and Schultz on board to support his new effort, then the FBI. The director wouldn't have to approve the plan, since he had already given the initial go-ahead.

At Scott's apartment in Alexandria, Matt suggested they make a video conference call to Schultz. Once they connected, Matt explained how he intended to use Karim to get to Dmitri by setting up a fake arms deal. His goal would be to force the man to come to the States to solve a problem that would arise. He would have to create one, but it would take some time. They had no viable way of chasing after him inside Russia, so they needed Dmitri to come to them.

"I've been thinking," Scott said. "Perhaps we also need a backup plan. You gave me the pictures of the man's office. I examined the photos you took with your phone in detail and I saw what I thought were two original paintings. I researched them and found out they were worth a fortune. The man must have a craving for that artist, and it's apparent from something else I found. Indeed, he might even be a collector of that particular artist. At least, I put it to you as an idea since I saw an email on his computer about the artwork. Let me show you." He pulled it up.

Stephan, I need a painting that my sources tell me is being advertised on the web. It is by Petro Alvazovsky. I want you to get it before it goes to auction. I'll pay twice what the owner wants. Just don't let it go up for auction. And if it does, get it at any cost. Dmitri.

"I think your people at the FBI should be able to break that down and find out who has it and where the painting is," Scott said to Matt.

"Why don't we get ahold of it and advertise it for sale?" Matt said. "He might take the bait, or he might not, but it might be worth a try. If he bites, we'll demand that it be picked up in person as a requirement for transfer and make that part of the sales agreement."

"Is that possible?" Scott asked. "I've never heard of such a thing."

"It is indeed," Schultz intoned from his image on the iPad. "I've used that ploy on some transactions to discover who's buying from me. They'll try to deceive you by sending a legal rep, but you can hold him to the terms of sale."

"So to get one of those paintings, we'll have to discover who has it for sale and procure it ourselves," Matt said.

"I did some looking for works by this particular artist and discovered that a painting by Petro Alvazovsky is going up for auction here at Sotheby's in two weeks. There are no other works of his for sale anywhere at present. They're valuable collector's items, and all the ones sold recently were outlandishly expensive. They won't negotiate before the auction now that it's been publicized."

"That may work in our favor," Schultz said. "If your man is a collector of this artist, he'll be searching for any of his works that come on the market. Let's get someone we know to buy it. It can't be me, because my history and business show that I never have indulged in art. I can, however, supply you with whatever funds you need."

"I'm broke, so it can't be me," Scott said.

"I believe I know someone who could fabricate the bona fides and the background to pull this off," Matt said.

"How are you going to do it?" Schultz questioned. His face moved in and out of the camera's eye on the iPad.

"I'm still an FBI agent, and I have access to some powerful computer friends who can fake all kinds of information. I believe the time has come for us to take advantage of them. I was afraid to employ them before because of the things we did and the places we went. Now we're engaged in an op that they are part of with Karim, so I can use them legitimately. We'll need to create someone who has a searchable background in the world of valuable paintings. I believe I know someone who can be created to be a convincing art collector," Matt said.

"That would give us another avenue to get Dmitri to come to us," Scott said.

"You can use my plane to deliver it if you need to. Is there anything else I can do?"

"Thanks," Matt said. "Did you find anything on that computer that you haven't shared?"

Before Scott could answer, Schultz interrupted, "I heard what you said about the names on the hit list, but Gertrude has been in the line of fire on two occasions. So I can't accept without some reservations that she isn't a target. We still need to protect her. She's now guarded by my men, and I recommend she stay there."

"I agree. I'll visit her in a few hours and tell her what we're doing," Scott said.

They ended the video conference. Matt took a seat on the sofa and looked at Scott.

"Is that all you're going to do there?" He smiled at Scott. "Again, is there anything else you found on the computer?"

"Get out of my house, you depraved character," Scott laughed. "Let me show you the material I uncovered."

"Are there more pictures?" Matt asked when he looked at the screen while Scott rolled through the take from Dmitri's computer. "These are all of an older lady, presumably his wife." More pictures scrolled by. "Wait." Matt pointed at the photo of a young lady. "I've seen her before."

There were more images of the same girl at various stages of her life, from a small child to a young woman at what appeared to be a university. Matt went to the corner and picked up the backpack. He had deposited it there on their return from Schultz's apartment following the trip to St. Petersburg.

"Pictures and papers," he said as he dumped the contents on the dining room table.

Matt discarded the two small-framed photos of an older woman, who he supposed to be Dmitri's wife. He learned that she had died a few years ago. He examined the framed picture of a young woman, perhaps around twenty. A guess would make her a favorite niece or something. He needed to know more about this girl who appeared in so many pictures on Dmitri's computer. He slid the cardboard backing from the frame and pulled the photo out, turning toward Scott with the picture in his hand.

"What you got?" Scott asked.

"Did you know that Dmitri had a daughter?"

"Never heard of one."

"Look at this." He passed it to Scott who looked at the picture and then turned the photo over.

"Good-looking girl. Look at this: 'To Dad, with all my love. Tasha, 12/2016.' In English. That's only a few months ago," Scott said.

"I never noticed before, but there's some writing etched in the stone wall behind her. Also, that tree, the one nearly out of the picture on the left, it looks like a palm tree to me. Are there palm trees in Russia?"

"Don't think so."

"Me neither. Now I need to get going. I'm heading downtown to see Liz and do a kiss-and-make-up with her before I dump this next job on her."

Matt stood, and so did Scott.

"Good-bye, Matt. By the way, what project will you give Liz?"

"I'm working on it," Matt said as he headed for the door.

29

———

FBI HEADQUARTERS

LIZ GARCIA FUMED, HER FACE ALMOST RED, AS SHE SAT TAPPING A pencil on her desktop. Matt had again failed to keep her informed of his actions, and the director held her responsible for running his black operations. She served as his control officer and supposedly kept him separate from the rest of the FBI. That aside, she harbored a deep-seated affection for this rogue. They had performed well as a team in the case of the Metro bomber, and again in rescuing that guy Schultz from a motel in Washington. She never allowed her feelings to show. She sometimes wished she could do something to let him see them a little. Right now, he remained devoted to Bridget, but perhaps that would change in the future.

Liz heard Matt open her door. Her office workspace occupied a small area next to the director's on the top floor. He entered, and Liz's eyes turned from warm to what could be described as two burning laser beams.

"I'm sorry," he said before she could get out a word. "I come bearing gifts." He slid the bouquet of flowers from behind his back.

"Oh, no, you don't, Matt Higgins." She took the flowers and tossed them into the trash can next to her desk. "I'm your boss, you have an obligation to keep me in the loop. You welched on that."

She turned back toward him, and he noticed some of the fiery intensity had departed her eyes.

"I came to ask you to forget that I didn't keep you updated every step of the way. I'm here to rectify that and to ask for your help in bringing a major arms dealer down."

"You can't sweet-talk me like that," she said. But she relented. "Tell me."

Matt brought her up to date on his venture to get Dmitri and his failure to apprehend his target. He then described the plan to use Karim to force Dmitri to come to the US.

The door to her office opened again. The director looked at Matt and signaled him to follow. Matt glanced to Liz, who gave him a knife-across-the-throat gesture.

* * *

MATT FOLLOWED THE DIRECTOR, WHO SHUT HIS DOOR AND TURNED to Matt.

"Where the hell have you been? Liz has been covering for you. I can tell she has. You disappeared for a few days. Where did you go?"

"I was following a strong lead on the man who set up the hit on Bridget, Scott and me. I've identified him as Dmitri Alexandrovitch, a Russian arms dealer who we encountered during the Savannah operation. He's the man who's responsible."

"How do you know?" the director asked in an unbelieving voice.

"We found the email in which he contracted for the hits."

"Found?" the director asked.

Matt chose to sidestep the question. "Now I want to use Karim to set up a sting operation on the man to get him to come here to the US." He knew this was his best plan, and the painting scheme would be his second option. He didn't want to confuse the director with multiple plans. He needed to get this one approved.

"You can't bring him down by yourself. You're asking me to release a known terrorist for you to use as bait. The DIA and CIA would crap in their pants if they knew. I would be hung out to dry after being forced to resign. No fucking way, Matt. Not possible."

The director shook his head to add emphasis to his decision.

"I know this'll work. We could build enough leverage to cause him to come here."

"What leverage? You can't bank on Karim. He hasn't given us a thing in the time we've had him. You think you can get him to do anything for you? I don't think so. Forget it. You don't have anything to use against Dmitri." The director pointed Matt to the door.

When he returned to Liz's office, she exhibited an "I told you so" look.

"You need to keep me informed at all times. I felt that you deliberately didn't answer your phone and didn't ask for any assistance for three days. So, you visited Russia. You owe me for not telling the director that you went off-reservation, but I think he guessed that I covered for you. You need to put this whole thing out of your mind. I know he told you to forget it."

"Thank you for the reminder. But now I need another favor."

"What? You have to be kidding." Her eyes rotated in their sockets.

"I'm not. I took a picture that I need analyzed. If your technical specialist, Libby Thompson, could use her skills like she did in the case we solved against the D.C. bomber, I might have another avenue to explore."

"Why do you want it run through our techs? This is going to cause me more grief. Remember, we're trying to keep you out of regular FBI channels. Make it good."

"I think it's Dmitri's daughter, and I'd like to know more about her. You never know, but this information might be the key to solving the problem of finding the bastard."

"Sounds good. Let's go." Liz got up and led him to where Libby worked. "Libby knows who you are, but she has no idea of your new role. Let's keep it that way."

They reached Libby's desk, and Libby stood up and gave Matt a hug. "I've been following your adventures. Liz keeps me posted. Sorry to hear about Bridget."

Matt felt the bile rise in his throat. He couldn't help himself. At most times, he could manage his reactions, but the image of Bridget lying in the alley reappeared without warning in his mind. He fought to regain control, and in a few seconds he accomplished it.

So much for Libby not knowing anything. He surmised from this that Liz apparently kept her informed as an old friend of his activity but hadn't enlightened her on his black ops for the agency. He would have to watch what he said.

Libby gave Liz a nod. "What brings you down to the bowels of technical?"

"I obtained a picture that I thought you might work your magic on." Matt handed her the photo, and he noticed his hands still shook from the emotional experience of a few seconds ago.

"This stays between us," Liz said in a low voice to prevent anyone else in the room from hearing.

"Got it," Libby said. "Give me a few hours. I suppose you want to know who this girl is, where she is, and what she had for dinner?"

"Skip the dinner for now," Matt said and gave her a smile. "We'll come back when you give Liz a call."

They returned to Liz's office. After they sat, Liz broke the silence that had dominated since they'd left Libby's office.

"What are you planning?"

"I'm going to set up Karim with an operation to market arms from Dmitri to terrorists here in the US, and you're going to get me the money I need to pull it off. I'll be the singular customer he sells to. No Fast and Furious screw-ups this time."

"I know the director gave tentative approval for your idea before you visited Karim, but I don't think he envisioned funding a large-scale sting, and he told you to forget it."

"He denied me permission to go ahead with my plan a few minutes ago. That's true, sort of," Matt lied. "We'd accomplish a great thing if I can pull this off."

"So what are you going to do now? I assume you won't quit because the director didn't give his approval. If you continue to go after him, you will piss the man off. Are you planning on taking

Dmitri alive? I want to know. I won't be a party to this whole thing if it's a vendetta operation for you. That is, presuming you're working on a way to get approved for this."

"I am, and it isn't. Sure, I'd love to kill him, but we plan to take him alive to extract what we can out of him. Satisfied?"

"Give me a few hours. I'll call you."

Matt left her office and went to a local Starbucks. He hated lying to Liz. Two times in almost as many minutes. He wanted to kill Dmitri. No question. He would learn all he could about the arms dealer's empire, but one way or another, he would terminate the man who had ordered Bridget's murder. The rage over Bridget's death started to boil up in his mind. It always brought on a feeling of emptiness in his soul. He took a deep breath and tried to relax. He regained control of his emotions, because he recognized the danger of not complying with the rules of the FBI if he wanted to walk away clean after this concluded.

An hour passed before his phone rang.

"Matt, get back here," Liz said without preamble. "Libby has something. She said she knows who the girl is and her current location."

30

———

DMITRI'S DAUGHTER

Matt gave Libby a smile when he had arrived at her desk. Liz trailed behind.

"What do you have for me?" he asked in his most pleasant voice.

"You sure know how to pick 'em. The young lady is Tasha Alexandrovitch. She's the daughter of Dmitri Alexandrovitch from St. Petersburg, Russia. She's currently on a student visa, so it would be a simple matter to locate her, and she is presently studying at the Savannah College of Art and Design."

"You're kidding," Matt got out. "Not Savannah again. But I do believe palm trees grow there."

"I never kid about my work. That is who and where she is. No mistake."

"I need another favor. Can you create a complete background with credentials to make someone a verifiable big-time art buyer?"

"Who's this for?"

"I'll let you know tomorrow."

Liz punched him in the back but didn't say anything. She must have guessed what he had planned for her.

"Piece of cake," Libby said. At that moment, a young man dressed in jeans and a sport coat came up to Libby's desk.

"Ready to go to lunch?" He had a neatly trimmed black beard with an accompanying mustache, and he wore a visitor's badge.

Matt only glanced at him before Libby got up to leave.

"Anything to help," Libby said. She departed with her lunch partner, and Matt headed away, followed by Liz.

He arrived outside the director's office with Liz.

"Am I the art dealer?" Liz queried.

"Yes, but that's the backup plan. I'll explain later. Now I need to get the director to change his mind."

The director stepped out of his office when he encountered the two of them approaching Liz's space.

"What now?" he asked.

"May I take a minute to explain something to you?" Matt asked.

They went into the inner office, and the director indicated for them to take a seat. "What is it?"

"I think I found the leverage to make my plan work. I need you to give me approval to take Karim out of the safe house and to set up a false arms operation. I know where the weak link in the target's armor is. He has a daughter, a student, here in the US. I can use that."

"How?"

"Perhaps it's better that you don't know," Liz added.

"I don't like it. I can almost visualize what you're going to do. It can't be sanctioned."

"Sir, you know what it would mean if we could crack the arms shipments to the US and the routes used to get them here. They must all use similar methods for delivery of the weapons, and we can round up more than this one with some new knowledge. We're only guessing now and are trying hit-or-miss ops against them, which haven't been entirely successful. I can fix that and arrest a major crime boss in one play."

"You can get us all fired," the director said and shook his head. "Now get out."

Matt returned to Liz's office. He noticed the flowers now resided on her desk.

"I think your plan is to pretend to break Karim out of our custody, set up an arms operation and capture this bigwig without Bureau assets. You're crazy," Liz said.

"Do you want this man taken down? Besides, the director didn't forbid it. He kicked me out of the office. He didn't say no this time." Matt smiled.

"I know that Dmitri tried to kill an FBI agent, murdered an innocent woman, and also attempted to kill two others," Liz answered. "So, yes, I want him taken down.

"To implement your plan, you'll need funding, and I control a sizable stash of money for operations. I'm willing to put myself on the line, and the director is going to be on a road trip to visit offices across the country for about two weeks. I can help you with Karim. But you had better make this work, or you're going to be viewing the world from a jail cell."

Matt stood and nodded in agreement.

"If word of this gets out, or Karim's departure is discovered, I can't help you. As the old saying goes, 'I'll deny all knowledge of this operation.' You will be on your own."

Liz stood and approached Matt. "So let me put it bluntly." She stood only a few inches from Matt's face. "If it fails, you're looking at a long prison sentence for helping a terrorist escape, because this agency will come after you as a criminal. If you're successful, and you capture the arms dealer, your man Karim is still going to Gitmo or a federal pen. Understand?"

Matt nodded.

"Those are the only possible outcomes for your operation," Liz said. "The piper has to be paid. Someone goes to prison. I don't want it to be you or me. Now go."

31

SCOTT EXPLAINS TO GERTI

SCOTT SNUGGLED UP AGAINST GERTI AFTER THEIR LOVEMAKING following lunch. The house they occupied, with the Schultz guards outside, nestled against a small rise in the Blue Ridge Mountains of northern Virginia. The view from the bedroom provided a spectacular sight, overlooking the floor of the lower Shenandoah Valley.

"We have to stop meeting like this." Gerti ribbed him as she said this. "I mean it, we need to get on with our lives. I feel like a nun in a convent secluded here, away from you."

"It won't be forever. I only want to be sure you're safe. Matt's working on a plan now, and I've made a backup one."

"What is it?" Gerti said with some excitement in her voice.

He explained his idea of using the painting to entice Dmitri to come out of Russia.

"Where are you going to secure such a valuable piece of art?"

"Matt's going to use the FBI resources to locate the person who has it—or, more likely, buy it at the upcoming auction. He then plans to resell it to Dmitri, since we know he ordered it purchased," Scott said.

"You're kidding. That's the plan?" Gerti asked.

"I think it has a chance of working," Scott said defensively.

"Sure," Gerti said as she got out of bed. "I'll make the drinks in a minute. You're staying here tonight." She gave him a kiss and headed for the bathroom.

Scott entered the living room, where he took a seat in a comfortable wingback chair and waited for his wife. She appeared and asked, "So how is this going to work?"

"At the auction, we'll outbid whoever is trying to get it for Dmitri and then offer to sell it for a profit. This will allow us to set up surveillance on the one who picks up the art. We'll follow it to Dmitri, and we'll nab him."

Gerti repeatedly shook her head. "No way. It's got too many moving parts. I learned from my father. K-I-S-S. Keep it simple, stupid."

Scott looked at her with deep respect, sensing her toughness. Then he placed a call to Matt, as Gerti declined to look at him.

"What's new?" Matt asked on answering.

"Nothing here. Do you have an art dealer yet?"

"Yes, but I need you now," Matt said.

"No way. I'm staying where I am until tomorrow."

"You'll miss the excitement."

"What excitement?"

"Are you coming?" Matt asked.

"Not this time. Tell me about it when you're done. I've got a marriage to work on tonight," Scott said and hung up.

32

———

MATT VISITS SCAD

MATT ARRIVED AT THE ADMINISTRATION BUILDING OF THE SAVANNAH College of Art and Design twenty minutes after noon. Upon presenting his credentials, he learned that Tasha Alexandrovitch had an exam ending in a half hour. Also, the receptionist informed him that he arrived on the last day before the summer break.

This presented Matt with a new problem. If the girl wasn't enrolled in school, she could go anywhere. That would not be a good thing from his perspective. He didn't want her going to Russia. His nascent plan required her presence here in the US.

He arrived at the hall where the girl was currently taking her exam and waited outside. Everything was in English at SCAD, and perhaps that explained the use of the language in the inscription on the back of the photo to her father. The hot weather made him want to remove his jacket, but his holster would be visible. So he suffered the heat and passed the time observing other students as they walked out of the building. Tasha appeared five minutes later.

"Excuse me. Are you Tasha Alexandrovitch?"

She stared at him with beautiful blue eyes, and he noticed she had a fully developed woman's body. After a few seconds, she seemed to make up her mind and nodded her head. "Who are you?"

"Would you walk with me a minute to get away from the entrance of this building? I'll show you my identification. But for now, I am a special agent with the FBI."

She stopped her initial steps to accompany him. "What have I done?"

"Let me assure you, I'm here to ask for your help." Matt's mind raced. He was making it up as he went along. "Please, let's go somewhere to talk."

They set off toward a coffee shop Matt had seen before on his way to the college, and after half a block, she stopped. "Let me see your ID."

He presented his creds, along with a business card, and let her examine them. "If you have any doubts, here's the number of the office in Washington. Feel free to call and verify my identity."

She reached into her purse and pulled out a cell. After a short conversation with Liz, she smiled at him. "You seem to be who you say you are. What is it you want from me?"

Her English was flawless—unaccented and clear. Matt veered off the sidewalk to enter one of the squares that adorned the downtown historic district of Savannah. He guided her to a bench situated on Ellis Square in the City Market area. They found an unoccupied bench and sat.

"We're having a major problem with certain Russian warlords—"

"I don't know anyone like that," she injected.

"I'm not accusing you of that. The assistance I require is with understanding the intercepts we have on their illegal activity."

"I would suggest you get my father to help you. He's a businessman in Russia and would be in a better position to assist than I am."

"Is that what your father does? What business is he in?"

"He has a large import-export firm. I don't know a lot about it, as he has never included my mother or me in any of his dealings. My mother died two years ago while I was here in school."

"I'm sorry for your loss," Matt said. This was an unexpected turn of events. The girl had no notion of the enterprises her father ran, and trying to get at the internal workings of the arms trade through her would undoubtedly prove useless.

"Again, I'm willing to help, but I learned one thing from my father —what's in it for me?"

Matt looked at her in appreciation of the intelligence he saw. "What do you want?"

"I want to stay in this country and pursue my art. Once my student visa expires, I must go back to Russia. I dearly want to remain here and work for some time before I have to return home."

"I know that you're out of classes for this year, so let me make you an offer. We found your application to work for a government agency online this summer. I want to offer you summer employment. Come and work with us. We've collected large amount of data on the people we're observing, and we would like you to help us. There's just one condition."

"What's that?"

"You will make no contact with anyone in Russia, or with anyone you know here in the US that has any Russian connections. We can't afford any inadvertent leak of anything we are working on. You will tell no one about the job you'll be doing. We have a house in Virginia that you'll use, and the work will be carried out there in secret with the assistance of some of our people."

"Not even my father?"

"Is that a problem?"

"Depends on what I get. Besides, sometimes I don't talk to him for months on end. But don't you have other Russian experts who can do this?"

"We do, but this is a special project—it's like an off-book program. That's the reason for this secrecy. It's scheduled to be over in early September and then you can return to your studies." Matt could sense that she was waiting for him to make her an offer.

"Give me a minute to talk to someone." He got up and walked a short distance and called Liz. The conversation lasted a short time.

"For your help and for your agreement to the conditions, I'll ensure you that you will obtain a permanent resident visa."

"You're shitting me. You can do that?"

"I give you my word and the word of the FBI. Do you agree?"

"When do I start?"

* * *

"Higgins, what the hell are you doing?" Liz queried when Matt redialed her.

"I need to get her on board. She might be of great value in getting Dmitri out of Russia. She doesn't know about his crimes, but from the little we know, he must love the girl. Besides, we've been looking for a Russian specialist. Now we got one."

"So you essentially put her in protective custody to keep her away from her father?"

"Sort of," Matt said.

"Sort of, my butt. You metaphorically kidnapped her."

"Well, maybe, if you want to look at it that way."

The director opened her door and stuck his head in. "I'm off for my trip. Keep Matt under control this time. Did you tell him yet?"

"No."

"When?"

"Much later. I don't want him distracted."

"Little harsh." He shut the door.

33

ART AUCTION

Matt occupied a seat in the rear of the room on the second floor of the Sotheby's office. He had arrived early and observed with great interest the men and women entering the room. The majority appeared to be businesspeople arriving from their downtown offices after the workday. He didn't notice anyone who attracted his particular attention or raised any concerns as he scanned each person who came into the room.

Liz arrived a few minutes before seven, the scheduled start time. He spoke into his mike. "See you, hear me?"

She nodded and walked forward to a seat in the center of a row halfway back, a placard with the number 33 gripped in her right hand. Matt assumed she had completed the registration and provided the identity check required for a bidder in order to obtain her paddle for bidding.

About a half hour into the auction, the painting they wanted appeared on the platform. He stood up in the back of the room. "That's it, isn't it?" Liz nodded without answering.

The auctioneer did his usual and initiated the bidding at two hundred thousand. Liz immediately held up her sign. Others started to raise the bid. Matt tried to move closer to Liz, but people had filled the side aisles when all the seats were taken.

This back-and-forth haggling went on for a few minutes as the auctioneer pushed and cajoled the price higher. Liz continued to bid until there seemed to be only one other person bidding for the prize, and he outbid her. The man sat almost directly behind Liz's seat. Matt heard the auctioneer blare out the next price increase, but Liz didn't respond to this higher amount. She didn't raise her paddle. Matt strained to see her, waiting in vain for her to act.

Nothing. No placard rose.

The auctioneer called the high price of four hundred fifty thousand. He repeated it three times and then sold the painting to the man sitting behind Liz.

"Liz, why didn't you bid?" He saw no movement and received no reply over their comms.

Matt saw the man stand and go to the back to pay. He hurried to Liz's location.

He plowed his way through the crowd occupying the side aisle and, with difficulty, approached the row where Liz sat in the center. She didn't look at him. In fact, she didn't move. He'd caused a commotion from the seated patrons as he pushed his way down the row of seats toward her. When he reached her chair, she didn't stir; no reaction to his approach.

Matt cupped her face. Her eyes didn't focus on him. He tried to get her to stand up, but she didn't attempt to help him. He put his hand on her neck and felt a strong pulse, but she didn't respond to his pleas to open her eyes. Panic set in as he pulled her up off the chair. He heard the click of something hitting the floor. Looking down, he saw a hypodermic needle.

Gently, he lowered her back to the chair.

He looked around for the man who'd sat behind Liz. At the back of the room, he spotted him heading toward the cashier's cage. He needed to get that man.

Matt tried to run after him, leaving Liz behind, but the chairs and people around him now impeded his pursuit. Liz slowly toppled to the floor without Matt's help in staying upright. Someone near her shouted, "Murderer!" on seeing Liz dropping over as Matt scurried after his target. The room turned into some kind of induced pandemonium by the shouts of the nearby people.

The way to the cashier proved to be packed with obstacles as the people in the back of the room headed toward the window where he could pick up his painting or leave instructions for its delivery. As Matt shoved his way toward the window, he saw the man heading toward the exit, having already paid for the painting.

"Stop that man," he shouted, pushing people out of his way. As he was about to get his hands on the object of his pursuit, a strong arm spun him around and put him in a body lock.

"Stand still, I'm detaining you until the police arrive."

With great effort, Matt rotated to face the security guard in a light blue shirt with a badge.

"You were assaulting people and two people tumbled to the ground because of your pushing. We'll wait for the cops."

"I am a cop. FBI. I'm chasing a criminal who is now getting away. Let me get my creds out." He could feel the man release him from his grip. He reached into his pocket and produced his creds for the security man.

"Sorry, man. What can I do to help?"

As he looked around, Matt noticed the purchaser of the painting now attempting to go through the exit. The man hurried at a medium pace and carried a large black bag over his shoulder, which Matt presumed contained the object he sought. The winner hadn't waited for the auction house to crate it, but must have insisted that as he owned it he could take it immediately.

After the security man released him and backed off, Matt swiftly moved away as if he had important business elsewhere.

Matt careened his way down the steps, to the consternation of the people he roughly pushed out of his way. Reaching the main floor, he headed for the front exit. After rushing through the door, he scanned the area. He saw the man with the case attempting to reach a limo that approached him. The car came at a fast pace and slammed on the brakes close to the man. The bidder must have called for the ride as soon as he'd secured the painting in his possession. Matt raced to within fifty feet and shouted, "Freeze, FBI. Don't move."

The man stopped, but he didn't freeze.

The painting slammed to the ground. This served as a brief distraction to Matt, but he recovered in time to see the man twirling toward him. The man's left hand came out from behind his suit coat, and the gun appeared with a speed that surprised Matt.

Art dealers, my butt, he thought as he dove forward. The first bullet impacted the car directly behind where he stood. Matt's weapon appeared in his right hand on the way to the ground. He landed, with his left shoulder impacting first. He rolled, acquired the target, and fired. The round went wide and the man returned fire.

Damn, this is bad. He needed to get off his next shot first. He used his training and fired without taking a sight picture on the target. He pulled the trigger a second time. His bullet hit the man, who careened against the limo and then tumbled to the ground near the painting.

Matt took a few seconds to regain his strength. He slowly pushed himself to his knees. Standing erect, he heard a car door open. Over the top of the limo, he could see the head of a man. Then he saw the weapon aimed at him. Being completely exposed with nowhere to hide, Matt knew his number was up. He could try to hit the small bull's-eye of the attacker's head presented over the roof of the car, but the odds were against him. The man simply needed to pull the trigger. Matt closed his eyes and brought up a mental picture of Bridget. He wanted his last thoughts to be of the woman he loved.

Two shots rang out and Matt waited for the pain as he knelt down. He waited. Nothing.

"Higgins, are you going to kneel there all night?" The voice of an angel—Liz's voice—now reached his brain.

"Are you hurt?" she asked.

He got to his feet and looked around. He felt alive and uninjured. A quick examination of his body proved it. He holstered his weapon. The painting lay beside the man he killed, and he retrieved it.

"Come around here," Liz said.

He rounded the back of the limo, where he saw the prone man who had had him dead to rights. He approached and bent down to turn the man over.

"What took you so long?" He smiled at Liz. "How did you get here?"

"That drug wore off, and all the shouting and pushing helped me recover. It must have only been to keep me quiet for a few minutes to silence my bid."

Matt and Liz looked down at the dead man.

"Holy shit," they both exclaimed on seeing his face.

34

LIBBY CONFRONTED

AN HOUR AFTER THE SHOOTING OUTSIDE THE AUCTION HOUSE, THEY arrived at Libby's apartment in the District of Columbia. She answered the door after taking a look through the peephole. In her pajamas, she appeared to be ready to go to bed.

"Come in. What brings the two of you here?" She invited them in with a hand gesture. "Please excuse my appearance. I wouldn't normally have opened the door this late, but I saw it was you. Can I get you something to drink?"

"No, thanks. We have a few questions." Matt moved in very close to her. "We noticed the other day that you went to lunch with a man."

"Yes, Victor, but he's not here now. He went out of town on business tonight."

"Does he live here?" Liz asked.

"Some of the time." She blushed. "Why all the questions?"

"We'll get to that in a minute, but right now I need you to tell me if you ever discussed with him what you created for Liz to act as an art dealer."

Libby looked away and down. "Not really." She rubbed her hands together rapidly.

"What does that mean?" Liz asked.

"The other night over drinks, I mentioned something about creating an art ID for an agent to buy a painting. I didn't give any names. Only small talk. You know."

"Did you happen to mention the date of the auction Liz told you about? The one you used to help craft the background for her?"

"I might have," she answered in a plaintive voice. Tears started to roll down her cheeks. "What have I done? Tell me. What is this all about?"

They informed her that Victor, who had posed as a limo driver, had attempted to kill them a short time ago. They had run his fingerprints and had confirmed his criminal past and his background as a member of the Russian mafia.

Libby looked as if she might faint. Her shock at the news appeared genuine.

The next day, after finding out from Libby the location of Victor's apartment, which wasn't the one listed on his driver's license, the FBI secured his computer. The recovered emails clearly showed Victor to be the one who had informed the known Russian arms dealer about the FBI's involvement in the sting operation at the auction.

Matt believed that somehow, through some Russian mafia connections, the word had gotten to Dmitri. Matt logically concluded that Dmitri still wanted the painting in spite of the warning, or possibly to test the validity of the information. Consequently, he remained willing to sacrifice some minions to check out the veracity of the source. Victor, someone he might not even have known, had paid with his life. All Libby's clearances were suspended pending final disposition of her case by the Office of Professional Responsibility.

35

KARIM IN BUSINESS

Matt sat in Liz's office, hanging his head. He didn't want to think of the future right then. Their plan to utilize the painting had now been relegated to the trash can. Nothing ever appeared to turn in his favor. He was no closer to getting Dmitri now than before they had gone to St. Petersburg. Nothing he did seemed to work. The art would have been the easy way; now he contemplated the hard way.

"I know we aren't as far along as you'd hoped to be by this time, but what are your options?" Liz asked.

"You know my opinion. There is only one." He paused. "We have to put Karim in play and hope he can provide us a way, even a contact, to get to Dmitri."

"God, I hate that option. So far we haven't risked much, but now we'll both be putting our necks on the line."

"You can look the other way. I won't tell you a thing about it from this moment on. You'll maintain plausible deniability."

"We've been together up till now. So don't pull that BS on me at this point. I'm already in too deep."

Matt still sat in contemplation, trying to map out the only option he saw.

"Higgins, move your butt out of my office. Do what you do best. Make it happen."

* * *

KARIM SAT IN HIS NEW OFFICE. HE RELISHED HIS NEW FREEDOM FROM the confining environment at the FBI safe house. This building provided the business space for the import-export business front on the first floor and a small apartment on the second. He knew that Matt Higgins wasn't dumb enough not to have the place bugged and under video surveillance. As part of his release, he had agreed to remain on the premises and not leave unless accompanied by Matt. He figured it an acceptable trade-off in comparison to the confinement he had endured at his previous location.

The desktop phone provided a link to the outside world, but he realized it too would be monitored. He did use the instrument to contact some of the people he'd met months ago. He remembered a few numbers and hoped they still worked. These guys had previously purchased weapons from various arms dealers, and he assumed some had used Mike Alexandro, the nephew of Dmitri Alexandrovitch. Therefore he believed they would be worth contacting. He needed to get the word out that he could supply arms if Matt's new plan was to succeed. At the same time, a different strategy from what Matt intended resided in Karim's mind.

Two days after his first phone calls, a rap on the door caused him to stir from his plan to escape. A man he recognized, named Husain, stood outside the office. When Karim opened the door, his guest towered over him at six foot six and weighed over three hundred pounds, his ruddy face covered by a thick black beard. The man didn't smile nor offer to shake his hand, but worst of all, he didn't give the Islamic greeting. Karim's guard went up.

"How can I help you?" Karim asked.

"You betrayed us."

Karim put his hand on the door.

"What are you talking about? I never did any such thing." Karim attempted to close the door. The big man used his foot to prevent its closing. "Go away, you're not welcome here."

"We can't trust you. You disappeared. Did you go to the FBI? We think you turned traitor, and now you show up trying to sell arms."

"You're out of your mind. I've been in hiding for over a month after that shoot-out in Savannah. I haven't picked up on any pursuit of me by the FBI, and I don't think they even know who I am. I got away clean, but I decided to lay low for a while. You should know that. So if you don't trust me, leave."

"I was testing you," the big man said. He took his foot away and Karim opened the door. The man gave the Islamic greeting and kissed Karim on both cheeks.

"That's better," Karim said with an audible sigh of relief.

"Do you really have access to arms? We're in need of someone with a connection to the Russians. We thought you might still maintain a way of getting new weapons."

"I do. What do you want?"

His visitor handed over a list. "We will pay top dollar for those items."

You will indeed, and the FBI agents watching this will have a field day tracking down your organization. "I'll call you when I receive confirmation that I can get your items and tell you the delivery schedule. Give me a number to use."

The man left after providing a cell number.

Karim took a seat in the office chair and waited. He felt confident Matt would check in on him in a few minutes. He had now made contact with some potential buyers. In the meantime, he visualized his eventual escape plan. The sole stumbling block remained money. He needed cash to make it work. He would ostensibly take in a large commission from the sale of the weapons to Husain, but that would never happen. The feds wouldn't allow it. So he needed to devise a way to obtain cash. The ringing phone interrupted his thoughts.

"Yes, Matt?"

"Good job. Keep up the good work." The line went dead.

His next visitor arrived an hour later, a man completely unknown to him.

"Karim, we learned you're back in business. Word travels fast, you know. We would like for you to procure some items for us."

Karim couldn't believe the speed with which the news of his new business had spread. That was what he desired. The more the merrier, as the FBI would be concentrating more on these guys and less on him. At least, that was his hope. The man in front of him took out a cigarette. Karim shook his head to indicate he didn't want any smoking in his office.

"Come outside with me, so I can have a smoke," his guest requested.

"By the way, what's your name?"

The man, in his early forties, wore jeans and a T-shirt, a black leather motorcycle jacket slung over his shoulder. "Zohair," the man replied.

Karim nodded his thanks and hoped the FBI hadn't bugged the outside of the place. After they lit up, Karim looked at his guest and asked, "Have you heard anything from any other Russian suppliers? I had to disappear for a month and wasn't able to keep up with any new developments. You understand?"

The man nodded. "Not much, but I did hear one tidbit."

"What would that be?" Karim asked.

"I hear that the uncle of Mike Alexandro has been spreading the word through people I know that he will pay a fortune to find the person who killed his nephew. The FBI never released any details. But no one knows anything about it as far as I can tell."

"Interesting. How is one supposed to get in touch, if I were to hear any information about that?"

"I got the number written down at my place. I'll drop it by in the morning with my list and you can tell me if you can obtain the items I need."

"I will give you a special price on your order if you can get me this by noon." The man nodded. After the deceived purchaser left, he reentered the office and let a wide smile appear on his face.

"Yes," he said aloud. In his mind, the plan to escape had solidified, especially since he knew who had killed Mike Alexandro. Now *that* information might bring him money and freedom. He had to get what he knew to Dmitri.

36

KARIM'S DECEPTION

THE NEXT DAY, SHORTLY BEFORE NOON, MATT SAT WITH LIZ, LOOKING out from a window across the street, and they discussed the current operation. Looking over to Karim's office, he carefully watched the man who called himself Zohair appear and enter through the front door of the small import-export business. Karim sat behind a gray metal desk, which held a phone with multiple line capability. The instrument had a speakerphone, and Matt used it to monitor Karim in the office. He had that number forwarded to his cell. They now monitored it while sitting across the street in a mom-and-pop restaurant drinking coffee.

"Do you have the list of items you want to order?" he heard Karim ask. Matt could see the man advance to Karim's desk.

"Yes and the thing you asked for," the visitor said.

"I am pleased. Wait, wait. What is the gun for?"

"You will tell me the name of the FBI agent who killed Dmitri Alexandrovitch's nephew. I want it, and I want it now or I'll kill you where you sit."

"I don't know who did it. I told you that I have been in hiding for a month. I got away before the shooting. Please put down the gun and let's talk this over."

"I want the name. I'll tell Dmitri. Tell me or you are dead."

Matt ran across the street. He flung open the door and pointed his weapon at the man. The man swiveled to face Matt, and at that moment Liz entered as the man fired. The sudden distraction by Liz coming through the door caused him to miss Matt on his first shot. He shot again at Matt, who dove for cover. Then he aimed his gun at Liz, who had drawn her weapon. Matt quickly rose and put two rounds into the man's chest, dropping him where he stood.

Karim crawled to where the body lay and recovered a piece of paper from his hand. Matt kicked the gun away from the man and moved to look after Liz. Karim started to hide the paper in his pocket with Matt's back to him.

"What are you doing?" Matt shouted at Karim, turning in time to witness the move by Karim.

"Nothing. Just making sure he is dead," came the response from Karim as he continued to search the man.

"Matt, we have to shut this op down. It isn't working like you planned," Liz said. "As soon as the local police arrive because of the gunshots, the whole thing is blown."

"Nobody in this part of town is going to call the cops because of a couple of muted gunshots. Let's wait a few minutes to see. In the meantime, I think Karim owes us an explanation." Matt went over to where Karim lay still on the floor and picked him up by the back of his shirt.

"Talk. The note he passed you, what's it for? You tried to pull a fast one. I want to know what it is, or you go back to solitary and probably Gitmo." Matt released him.

"I still think we need to close this operation down," Liz said in a determined voice.

"We have to keep going. Karim is the only person who can pull this off. He has to be in play." Matt walked over to where Karim now stood.

"I think I must tell you something. I don't want to go back into custody or to Gitmo."

"You conniving little bastard. What are you trying to pull?" Matt demanded.

"When I went outside yesterday with him, he told me that he learned that Dmitri is willing to pay a lot of money to get the name of the person who killed his nephew. I asked him to give me the number. That's what's on this sheet of paper," Karim said as he passed the note to Matt.

"Text and inform whoever gets it that you know the name and address of the person who killed Dmitri's nephew in Savannah. You will only give that information to Dmitri himself in person."

"Are you sure this is a good idea?" Liz asked.

"I think this might be the fastest way we can get at Dmitri, and it's bait to lure him here," he said.

"You mean you're the bait, as I assume you'll have Karim tell him it's you."

"Precisely," Matt said with a smile.

"Remember that in Savannah, I wasn't the one who shot his nephew, but he has no way of knowing anything different. Now Karim here is going to tell him I did it."

In less than a minute after Karim sent the message, a text arrived on Karim's cell. "Accept offer, money will be transferred on delivery of name."

Matt took the phone and texted back, "Not acceptable, come to my location and get the name after you hand me the money."

"Accepted," came the reply.

37

DMITRI'S DAUGHTER

Scott called Schultz and told him that his daughter was continuing to recover and was almost completely mended.

"Anything else, Scott? I appreciate your keeping me updated."

"Nothing really. We've been working with Dmitri's daughter. Mark has her in something like protective custody."

"That's interesting," Schultz said. "This is the first I've heard of it."

"I guess with all that's going on, we didn't mention it, since she's in a secure place."

"Where is she?"

"At a farm in northern Virginia."

"Come on, Scott, exactly where are you keeping her?"

"Since you've supported us from the start and already spent a lot of money to get us this far, I guess it'll be no problem." He gave him the address that Matt had given him in case he needed to go there.

"You take care. Thanks for the update." Schultz hung up.

Scott sat and considered the conversation. He had only wanted to be in touch with his father-in-law in order to build a good relationship with him. He thought that by his doing so, he and Gerti would establish a closer connection with her father.

Something bothered him now; Schultz had shown an unusual interest in Tasha's location. What difference did it make to him where she was staying? Maybe he'd made a mistake in telling him about the daughter. He decided to ask Matt for his take on the conversation. He drove to the house where Gerti currently stayed before he called Matt.

* * *

ON HEARING SCOTT'S REPORT OF THE CONVERSATION WITH SCHULTZ, Matt shouted over the speakerphone, "Are you kidding me? Why did you do such a dumb thing?"

Gerti heard the commotion and came into the room.

"What's going on?" she asked.

Matt took a minute to bring her up to date.

"Oh no. Not good," Gerti said. "I'm afraid with that information, Father will go after her. You see, he now holds Dmitri responsible for the attacks on me."

"The message he read says you aren't on the hit list," Scott said.

"Believe me, he thinks I was a target, and as close as some of the events we experienced came to ending my life, I think he may have a point, from his perspective. I know him. He wants revenge."

"I'm always trying to build a better relationship with your father. I thought keeping him in the loop would help us," Scott said.

"I know, but you don't know how he thinks," Gerti said.

Matt again focused the conversation. "Scott, you're probably closer to Tasha than I am. Go get her."

He then said to Gerti, "Could you get away from your house to be with Tasha? It would mean leaving there and going without your father's protection, but I'll have Liz get a safe house ready for you."

"I can do that. Scott will come with me," Gerti finished.

"Sure," Scott said.

"Scott, go get Tasha at our safe house. Gerti, when Liz texts you the location for the new place, enter it into the GPS. It may be nothing, but I'd rather have her safe than in Schultz's hands, where he would probably try to force Dmitri to come to a place where he would kill him, if Gerti's correct about his thought process. If that happened, he'd likely kill the girl too. We can't let that happen. He has the means to do it and to make it disappear."

"Heading there now."

"I'll head to the new safe house and wait for Scott," Gerti said. "My car's here and I can slip past Father's men."

"Scott, you have that second phone I gave you for us to use. Give it to Tasha, and tell her we're the only ones who will contact her on it."

Before Matt ended the call, Gerti said, "I think we are right about Father's intentions. He is fully capable of doing that. Especially if he thinks I'm in any danger."

* * *

GERTI SNUCK OUT AND DROVE AWAY IN HER CAR. SHE RECEIVED THE text from Liz and put the location into her GPS. As she headed for Tasha's proposed new location, she spent a few minutes thinking about her current predicament. While driving, she realized that she and Scott had a great plan for the rest of their lives. After she had become pregnant, they had discussed how they would raise the child and what they wanted to do in the future.

Now, with the events going down with Dmitri, his daughter, and the actions her father might take, it all appeared to be in jeopardy. She'd always feared becoming like her father, but now she realized that in so many things, she thought the same way he did. She would probably do the exact same thing he would in regard to Dmitri's daughter. Fear of what she might become, might already have become, now plagued her thoughts. She didn't want to become her father, no matter how much she imitated him in many respects. How would she find her true course, her path with Scott, her relationship with her father?

So many questions, with no clear answer in sight. She knew the right thing to do would be to save the Russian girl and make sure she remained unharmed. She decided to concentrate on one thing at a time.

She figured it would be twenty minutes before she reached new safe house—plenty of time to try to unhinge herself from her father's thought process.

38

DECISIONS

AFTER RECEIVING THE TEXT MESSAGE FROM KARIM, DMITRI AGAIN TRIED to contact his daughter. He had had no success for weeks attempting to get in touch with her, but had chalked it up to a young woman enjoying her vacation from school. She generally called back within a few days, or maybe a week, but not this time. Something might have happened to her, or worse. He would certainly have received a notice by the State Department if anything really bad had occurred.

This Karim wanted to meet him personally to give him the information on who had killed his nephew. He didn't want to talk with the snitch, but this might be the opportunity he needed to go and visit his daughter.

At that moment, he received a call from the Robocop.

"What do you want?" Dmitri demanded, attempting to control the conversation.

"You know what I want. You haven't completed your contract. I know who you are, but you don't know me. Perhaps it is time to employ someone else to handle it." The modulated voice couldn't sound threatening, but it conveyed exactly what the speaker intended. "You get no more money unless the contract is completed in two days."

Dmitri hated to be threatened by anyone, and especially by this buffoon, who couldn't even do his own dirty work.

"It will be done," he said and hung up.

Dmitri took a few seconds to contemplate his next move. Unbeknownst to the caller, he knew the caller's true identity. At that moment, he determined that Mr. Robocop needed to be eliminated.

In the end he thought it best to go to America and kill the man who had murdered his kin, and he would throw in the other buffoon for good measure. Since he knew who had contracted him for the hit on Bridget, Matt, and Scott, he decided to silence the man as protection for himself. He possessed the means and the will to get them both accomplished.

He looked at his security man standing inside the door of his office. This man had protected Dmitri for years and went everywhere with his boss. "Andreas, pack your bags. We are off to America today. We'll take my jet."

* * *

SCHULTZ HUNG UP THE PHONE AFTER TALKING TO DMITRI. HE clenched his fist and pounded it into his left hand again and again. This had to end, and soon. He let his mind go back over the things he had done to see if he had done something wrong.

His interest in the Donavans had all started when he'd learned that Bridget Donavan had let his son die while on a combat operation in the Middle East. True, he'd later heard that she might not have been solely to blame, but in his mind, she remained responsible for the death of his son.

During a subsequent episode, Scott and Bridget had sought to acquire the Bible of Constantine. Bridget had saved his life in this encounter, but then ripped him off for five million immediately afterward. This still left a bad taste in his mouth.

Due to some unforeseen circumstances, Matt and Scott had fortunately escaped Italy and later Russia without a scratch. In both places, they'd suffered attacks on their lives that he'd orchestrated.

Then his thoughts turned to his precious Gertrude, who would give him a grandchild. He'd never thought she would marry, but now she seemed to be on the track he had always planned for her, and she would soon take over the running of the business. She had a mind that mirrored his in almost all respects. He could see himself in her, and in time she would also. She had the same dominant streak in her character that he did.

The need for his personal action in this matter appeared to be approaching. He no longer could sit on the sidelines and attempt to allow others to do his bidding. The time had arrived for him to do some things for himself.

39

TASHA'S SAFE HOUSE

SCOTT ARRIVED AT TASHA'S LOCATION, WHERE HE KNOCKED ON THE door and waited for her to open it. When she did, she stared at this man she had not seen before.

"Tasha, my name is Scott Donavan. I work with Matt Higgins, who sent me here to take you to a different safe place. Pack your bags —we've learned that someone has probably discovered this location and is coming to kidnap you. Please hurry, and I'll wait for you."

"Yes, Matt called, and I started packing immediately. Let me run upstairs and finish. I fear I have a lot of stuff, especially books," Tasha said. She left the door open and ran to her bedroom. In about four minutes she returned carrying one suitcase and set it down near the door.

"Scott, could you go up and bring down my other suitcase? I really can't pick the thing up with all the books."

"Can do, but I want to give you this cell. It's a phone that's connected directly to Matt and myself, and we use it for our internal personal communication. It has encryption on, so you don't need to worry about what's being said when you talk to us. Please put it in a safe place."

"No need, I already have an iPhone." She pulled it out of her purse and showed him.

"I understand, but this is a separate means of communication, so please stash it somewhere and we will use it to communicate with you, and you with us."

"Sure," she said. She went over to her suitcase and placed the phone into it, replacing her iPhone into her purse.

Scott ran up to the second floor, where he saw the suitcase inside the bedroom door. He went over to pick it up. As he raised the bag off the floor, the contents spilled out.

"Damn," he said. He bent over and started placing the items back in. Most of these were books, and he eventually got them all back in and then zipped the suitcase up. He lifted it up and at the same moment he heard the screech of tires outside. Forgetting about the heavy suitcase, he rushed for the stairs.

"Tasha," he screamed.

He reached the bottom of the steps and didn't see Tasha's suitcase, but worse, he didn't see Tasha. He raced over to the door and looked up and down the street. A car sped away and disappeared around the corner before he even got a good look at it.

"Damn, damn, damn," he shouted as he grabbed for his phone.

* * *

"Scott, slow down," Matt ordered as Scott spewed forth information so fast he couldn't make heads or tails of the man's blabbering. "Tell me what happened. Take it easy."

Matt put him on speaker so Gerti could hear. He had joined her at the safe house. Scott spoke again in a much more coherent manner and ended with the car disappearing around the nearby corner.

"I should have thought about it earlier. As soon as you told me that Father knew about Tasha, I knew his most likely move consisted in grabbing her to get at Dmitri, since he still believes that man had me as a target of the assassin," Gerti said.

"I got here as fast as I could," Scott said.

"No one's blaming you. We need to regroup and figure out how to save that innocent girl. Gerti, any ideas where he might take her?" Matt asked.

"No, because Father hasn't fulfilled his promise to fill me in on all the things in the company that I'm not aware of. I'll call him to see if I can find out anything."

"Don't waste your time. He won't tell you anything now that he's taken her," Scott offered.

"Wait a minute," Gerti said. "I got a text from Father. He's coming here this afternoon. He doesn't say why, but I bet it has to do with the girl. He wants to be here to use her to get Dmitri."

"I bet it is," Matt said.

"Scott, come back and pick me up. I want to be with you from now on. I'm sick of this prison I'm in. It's time we aren't separated anymore."

"On the way, but be careful. We don't know what those guys' instructions are."

Liz's number appeared on Matt's cell, and he realized she must need to talk with him. He told them he needed to take the call.

"Liz, I got bad news."

"You go first," she said.

"We think Schultz has kidnapped Dmitri's daughter."

"How the hell did that happen?" she asked.

Matt told her what they knew and what they suspected. He finished with, "What do you have for me?"

"Last night, Dmitri Alexandrovitch arrived in the United States."

40

DMITRI'S ARRIVAL

DMITRI'S GULFSTREAM 650 HAD ARRIVED IN TETERBORO, NEW JERSEY, where it cleared customs and refueled. After that, it flew on to Manassas Regional Airport in Virginia. The plane touched down amid clear skies and a mild temperature. The tower directed the plane to a remote section of the field with what looked like an abandoned old building that might have been the previous space of the FBO (fixed base operations). An access road wound its way to the border fence with a small gate allowing entry with a card swipe.

Dmitri met with the provided driver, Yuri, as soon as his jet landed near Washington, D.C. Yuri, in his early twenties, sported long black hair, with tattoos showing above his shirt collar. The man drove the black SUV, which took Dmitri and his personal bodyguard, Andreas, to the Hilton Hotel. He liked to take a rest after any long flight. Yuri drove them to downtown D.C. In the morning, he delivered them to the address that Dmitri provided.

Dmitri decided the time had arrived to visit the man called Karim and get the information on who had actually killed his nephew. He checked his briefcase, inside which the bribe money rested. He didn't really plan on giving a snitch that much cash, but he would if it became necessary. He placed a call to Karim.

"Are you the man who will tell me who killed my nephew?"

"If you are the man who has my five hundred thousand, then I am he."

"See you soon." Dmitri ended the call and placed another call to Yuri's boss. This man's family had been friends of his family from his early childhood. The man he called had left Russia as a young man, with Dmitri's father's help, to set up a new branch of the family business in America.

"Hello, Artur. I believe your father told you I would be contacting you," Dmitri said.

""Yes, he did. It is a pleasure to hear from you, Dmitri Alexandrovitch. What can I do for you?"

"I will need five to eight well-trained men. Is that a problem?" He heard the negative reply and said, "I'll call you in an hour and tell you the target and the location. There will be additional instructions. Altogether it will be one, maybe two days' work. Text me your expenses and you'll be compensated before we begin."

"Pleasure to do business with you. No problem, they will be available on your call," Artur responded and ended the connection.

Dmitri waited only a few seconds before the bill arrived, and he transferred the money immediately. He sat back and relaxed with a smile on his face.

His first aim would be obtaining the name from this Karim, and the next would be Schultz. They would both be dead before he left to return home, maybe even later today.

* * *

MATT ANSWERED THE PHONE CALL FROM KARIM, WHO HAD BEEN TOLD to call Liz on duty near his location if anything happened.

"Why are you calling me?" were the first words out of his mouth when he answered.

"Listen. He's on his way here. He said he would be here soon."

"I'm on my way. Hang up and call Liz," Matt ordered.

"No, wait. I need to tell you something."

"What?"

"I'm afraid he will kill me if he gets here first."

"Why?"

"Well, I called the number to tell him I really knew who killed his nephew. I failed to tell you he offered me five hundred thousand dollars. I now realize he would never pay that kind of money to a snitch, so I'm dead," Karim said.

"You son of a bitch. So, you were going to use the cash to escape and set yourself up in a new life. Now, it looks like someone will solve my problem for me."

"Please, Matt, he'll kill me for sure. You gotta help."

Matt hung up the phone and called Liz. He would be there in ten minutes. She was already there observing Karim. The little weasel had really done it this time. Matt believed what the man had said. After Dmitri got the name, he would, without reservation, kill the informant. There would be no reason to leave a loose end around who could obtain some favors by contacting the FBI or locals and ratting out a Russian crime lord visiting the USA. That couldn't be allowed, so Karim had to go.

He looked at his phone, which gave an unusual sound. The call came from the cloned one that Tasha had. Matt thought that if they took her, they would certainly have taken her phone. Maybe one of the kidnappers used it. He picked it up to listen to the conversation. He soon found out that she had dialed her father.

"Hello, Papa," she said.

41

—————

TASHA KIDNAPPED

"Tasha, where are you? I've been so worried. Are you all right?" Dmitri couldn't see it, but before she answered, Tasha covered her face with a blanket to mask her voice.

"No, Papa. I've been kidnapped. I believe they work for a man named Schultz, as that's the name I heard the guard say on the phone to someone he reported to. I had forgotten about having this phone that I put in my suitcase. They didn't search it, only my purse. They took my iPhone when they grabbed me. I've been too scared to do anything until now. They locked me in this room on the second floor. There are two guards in the house. I looked out the window and didn't see anyone walking around outside. It's too steep to jump out. I'd break a leg."

Dmitri almost crushed the instrument in his hands. He would kill the bastard for this attack on his family. He told himself to calm down. The first priority was to get his daughter back. Two men, Yuri and Andreas, his personal bodyguard, accompanied him, but Artur remained on contract. Best to employ local assets to do the heavy work. He would be there to rescue his daughter.

"Where are you?" he asked.

"Wait a minute. I think I can use this phone to get my location." In a second she came back. "Got it." She gave him the address of her location. He wrote it down in a notebook from his pocket and tore out the page. He handed to the driver and said, "Take me there."

The driver nodded and retrieved the paper. Dmitri called Artur to request the three reinforcements he believed would be required for retrieving his daughter. That gave him four shooters, three from Artur and his own security man, Andreas, with the driver staying in the car.

"How long?" he asked Artur.

"Thirty minutes."

* * *

Matt looked at the location on his GPS. He could be there in less than ten minutes. He didn't know how far away Dmitri was, but he needed to get the girl free immediately in case Schultz did something stupid. He had no backup here, and taking on Dmitri in an open fight wasn't in his best interest. If he could get the girl, then he would have a chip to play in the game. He needed personal access to Dmitri to find out the answers to his questions.

Since Dmitri didn't know who had shot his nephew, it didn't make sense that he had put a contract out on them on his own. He must be doing the job for someone else. That someone would be the end of the line, the target of his vengeance. He now knew that he needed Dmitri to provide the last piece of the puzzle.

With Dmitri this close, having the girl would give him the upper hand. He would make sure the daughter remained safe in his custody as soon as he could get her away from her captors.

"Yes, Matt. What do you need?" Scott asked on answering Matt's call.

"I have the girl's location. She called her father and gave it to him. That cloned phone she has is slaved to mine and I heard it all. He's on his way to her now, but I'm ahead of him. I plan on getting to her first.

When I do, I need you and Gerti to help me with her. I'll bring her to the new safe house."

"We'll be there. Anything else?"

"Not now."

42

___

TASHA'S RESCUE

Matt raced to the girl's location. When he saw the house, he realized there was no easy way to sneak up on it. The building stood on a half-acre lot with a manicured lawn extending from the house in all directions. Anyone approaching would be seen by a guard in front or back of the house. He concluded that if these were Schultz's men inside, they were fair game since they had kidnapped the Russian girl.

On looking around from inside the car, he observed an elderly lady slowly walking her dog down the street. She would pass directly in front to the house on her present course. If these guards had been here last night and this morning, they would have seen the woman previously and probably wouldn't give her or the dog a second glance.

Matt jumped from the car. He had parked it about three hundred feet from the property and under a tree, where it should be out of sight of anyone looking out of the house. He hurried to catch up with the lady, who walked her dachshund on a pink leash.

"Excuse me, ma'am. I can't help but notice that your dachshund is well behaved."

The elderly woman slowed her pace and looked at Matt, but

continued on her stroll. She wore a blue Georgetown sweatshirt with matching sweatpants. Her feet were adorned with pink tennis shoes.

"Thank you, young man. She's old like me, so we walk rather slowly." He walked beside her now and they proceeded to pass along the sidewalk that ran directly in front of the house. "Haven't seen you around here before. Where are you from?"

"I'm going to visit this house right here," Matt said as they approached the walk leading up to the front of the house. In the window he observed a man watching them, but after seeing the old lady, the watcher turned away. Matt assumed the man had lowered his guard at the sight of the old lady, as he'd hoped.

"Nice talking to you," Matt said. He smiled at her and gave a slight wave as he turned and ran at full speed toward the door.

As he approached, he pulled his Glock, immediately firing at the lock on the door. He plowed into the door and it gave way. He dove low, and off to his side, he noticed the man from the window was caught by surprise. In the few seconds it took for him to reach for his gun, Matt put two rounds into his head. No question of surviving that.

He heard a name being called from upstairs. Matt guessed it belonged to the dead man. Since he had never heard the man say anything, he couldn't try to imitate him with pain in his voice as if he'd been wounded. A deception he used on some occasions, but not for this situation. So he coughed loudly and moaned like a wounded man might.

"Hang on, Bill," the man said as he ran down the steps. Matt realized these guys were definitely the second string. No trained operative would ever allow him to get away with crashing the door, because he should have been stopped long before reaching it.

Matt heard the creaking of the stairs and concluded that the man coming down weighed a good amount from the pounding he inflicted on the steps. Matt moved with speed to place himself beside the living room wall, which would cover his presence while allowing the man descending the steps to see his fallen comrade as soon as he entered.

The man rounded the corner, and in a flash Matt saw that his initial assessment of the situation proved correct. The man weighed over two hundred and fifty pounds. A revolver protruded around the corner ahead of him.

"Freeze, FBI," Matt shouted.

Matt heard the cocking of the hammer as the overweight man turned and swung the weapon toward Matt.

"Drop it," Matt commanded.

The weapon continued on toward his position with no interruption. The man apparently intended to kill him. Matt fired two rounds into the man's head. He didn't have time to do anything different. He needed to get the girl and leave the place before Dmitri arrived.

He ran upstairs and opened the only door that remained closed on the second floor. Tasha sat on the bed and looked startled on his entry.

"Matt? Did my father send you?"

"We have to go before more of Schultz's men arrive. Let's go," he urged.

He preceded her down the stairs as fast as he could. She followed him and he guided her as they hurried up the street to his car. When they were seated inside the vehicle, he started the engine. Before he could shift it into drive, he saw a minivan speeding in from the opposite direction and approaching the front of the house.

In his rearview mirror, he noticed two black SUVs that flew past him while he sat in the car. The SUVs rolled up and six men got out. The minivan he'd observed approaching from the opposite direction had stopped. The occupants of the van exited the vehicle with lightning speed and opened fire on the exposed men from the SUVs, who were grabbing for their guns. The hail of automatic fire ripped into the men in the open and some went down. The remaining men in the van jumped out and ran toward the house.

"We need to leave. Whoever they are, they're going in to get you. I don't know whose side they're on. We'll find out who won later. Not a good time to confront aggressive shooters," Matt said to Tasha as he shifted into gear and did a U-turn in the road.

"Where are we going?"

"To a safe house."

"So far your safe houses haven't exactly worked out," Tasha scolded.

Before he could react, Tasha held the phone to her ear and announced, "Papa, I've just been rescued. He is—"

43

CONFRONTATION WITH DMITRI

Matt grabbed the phone and shut it down before he gave it back. He couldn't have Dmitri knowing about him at this time. He had to formulate other plans, but at the moment, he didn't know what they were. First, he had to get Tasha safely into Scott and Gerti's hands. Next, he needed to reach Karim before Dmitri did. He assumed that one of the groups in the firefight belonged to Dmitri and was trying to rescue his daughter, and the other to Schultz, who was attempting to use her to get to Dmitri for some reason he didn't comprehend.

"Why did you do that?" Tasha asked.

"I need to keep you safe. I found you when you used that phone, and anyone listening to you talk on it would acquire the same information you would give him. We don't need another bloodbath. I'm taking you to a safe place, and we'll work out how to contact your father. You know he's nearby, so it shouldn't be a problem. Let's be careful for now." At least that logic might make her go along with his evolving plan.

Matt drove to meet Scott and Gerti at the location Liz had texted him. Once he reached them and delivered Tasha into their care, he raced off to get to Karim before Dmitri determined the attempt to rescue his daughter had failed. Then he would continue to go after the snitch while he attempted to find his daughter. Matt wanted to plan a trap for him at Karim's place. If he could get there first and set up inside with Liz covering the outside, he might take Dmitri when he came in to confront Karim. At least that constituted a basic action plan. He drove in excess of the speed limit to arrive before Dmitri, and to set a trap to ensnare him. Few plans, however, survived first contact with the enemy. Matt realized that truism from experience in the Middle East.

* * *

DMITRI SHOOK HIS HEAD IN BEWILDERMENT AT THE RESULTS OF THE GUN battle he watched from a block away. The Russians had been mauled, but they had fought Schultz's men to a standstill before his three men had fallen, with Andreas the only one to escape. Both sides had lost three or four before the gunfire ceased, and the remnants gathered up the wounded and dead before speeding off. No one came out of the house. Dmitri knew that his daughter couldn't be there if no one had emerged from the building after the loud firefight, especially since Schultz's men had actually won.

Dmitri ordered Yuri to take him immediately to the address he provided. They left for Karim's location as soon as Andreas reached his car.

He called Artur and gave him a situation report. He knew the man's men were dead, but he needed him to have more operatives available for planned future needs. He requested two men immediately to meet him at Karim's address.

"I can get them there in less than ten minutes."

"Good. I'll be there at that time. Have them prepared for action on my arrival." Dmitri ended the call.

He arrived at the address and noticed two men pile out of a car parked opposite the building. Now he would find out who had killed his nephew, and use these new assets to eliminate that person. Things were now looking good. Dmitri smiled as he exited the car. He walked over to meet Artur's men to give them his instructions.

"You"—he pointed at one of the men, who looked to be the biggest and strongest—"go in front of me into the store. Have that rifle ready, but do not fire unless I tell you or someone fires at you."

The Russian mobster nodded his understanding. Dmitri pointed to the other. "Stay outside and provide cover. I don't trust this man. I have a feeling there may be some FBI involvement, and this target might be under surveillance." The man nodded. Dmitri wasn't sure about the connection to the FBI, but he had found out from a source that one of the men who had come to his home in St. Petersburg did have some kind of connection with the FBI. He believed in always being prepared for the worst.

Heading for the entrance to Karim's place, they crossed the street.

44

KARIM'S OFFICE

Looking out the front window, Karim could see three men approaching as they traversed the street. It had to be Dmitri. He dialed the one-touch number to reach Matt, and on hearing his voice, he shouted, "They are here." He placed the phone on his desk without disconnecting when the first man pulled the front door open.

If this went well, he started to believe, he could actually get the money before Matt arrived. Then he could really escape. His mind danced with that delightful thought. He had covered up his ultimate plan by playing ball with the FBI, and in keeping with his escape plan, he had always kept Matt advised to allay any suspicions that might arise. At present, the best course of action would be to tell Dmitri about what had happened in Savannah and hope he received the money. With the cash, he could flee out the back door and disappear into the jihadist underground in the States. That now became his total focus.

His hands were trembling a little, and he could feel his heart rate increase. The moment had arrived, the one he'd waited for since the FBI had grabbed him in Savannah. He had engineered his own escape, and he would use the opportunity to his advantage. In his mind, he had covered himself no matter which way this played out.

He stood up to meet the men entering the store and simultaneously placed a wide smile on his face. Yes, he could pull this off before Matt arrived.

* * *

THE GUARD EXITED THE FRONT OF THE VEHICLE AND OPENED THE DOOR to Karim's place for Dmitri. He stepped into the office, remaining slightly to the right side of his principal. From there he had a clear line of sight on Karim. Dmitri carefully eyed the man in front of him and decided he could be a dangerous threat in many circumstances, but there appeared to be no weapon on the man, and none were visible anywhere near him. Dmitri proceeded with his question.

"Do you have the name of the person responsible for the murder of my nephew?"

"Yes, I do." The man looked directly at him when he responded. Dmitri estimated that this individual could be a fearsome opponent in any case. He did not know of Karim's background in the Revolutionary Guard of the Islamic Republic of Iran.

"You demanded that I come here in person to deliver you the money. Quite an unusual request, I must say. How do I know the information you will provide is legitimate?" He noticed his guard move further to the side for a clearer shot at Karim if needed, with his semiautomatic slung over his shoulder. His movements would keep Dmitri out of any danger of being in his line of fire. *Smart man, a lot better than the previous hires Artur sent*, Dmitri thought. He might have further use for this man.

"First of all, in Savannah, I saw what happened because I was there. And more importantly, if I lied to you, I would be a dead man. You know what I look like. Your men could find me anywhere I tried to hide. The information is accurate. And my money?"

"In this case," Dmitri said, placing it on the desk and opening it, "is half of the money I agreed to pay. The other half will be delivered by cashier's check to whatever address you provide, once I obtain what I want. I think that is a reasonable arrangement for conducting business with someone I don't know. Now, who killed my nephew?"

"Matt Higgins," he said as Matt had instructed him.

* * *

As Matt raced to Karim's location, he called Liz.

"Matt, the men are here. Two went into the office and one is acting as an exterior guard," she said when she answered.

"I know. Get into position to take out the outside man. I'll go straight in and get the ones inside."

"That's your plan?"

"It's the best I can do on the fly. You have anything better?"

"Damn it, it's too late to call for backup. I'll be ready to take him out. He has a weapon in his hand now."

"When you see me drive up, take him down, no hesitation, and then cover me as I go in. Thirty seconds."

"Got it," Liz said and closed the connection.

The director would have a hissy fit over this type of takedown, but he couldn't let Dmitri escape. He believed someone else had hired Dmitri to put out the contract on him and Bridget and if it wasn't his initiative to start with, Matt needed to know who paid him to do it.

Now only a half a block away from the store, Matt prepared himself mentally as best he could. On reaching the front door of the import-export business, he slammed on the brakes, pushed open his door, and got out, pulling his weapon as he did.

"Hey, you," he heard coming from a man rushing toward him with a weapon drawn.

Two shots rang out, and the man tumbled forward. He turned and saw Liz rushing toward the downed man and kicking the weapon out of his reach.

Matt swung rapidly back toward the entrance. He thought he heard Liz running behind him. He figured she would stop outside to secure his back as he plowed in. He flung the door open. A man with a semiautomatic rifle swiveled it toward him and opened fire.

45

DMITRI'S DELIGHT

Dmitri stood dumbfounded at the revelation that Matt Higgins happened to be the one who had killed Alex Alexander. Reluctantly, he had come to believe that this informant knew what he was talking about. It made sense to him now, but the best part of the entire operation was the fact that Schultz would pay him back the money he would give Karim, and then he would have the satisfaction of exacting his own vengeance on Matt Higgins. He smiled at the realization of his double victory. He would kill the murderer of his nephew, and get paid for it by the supposedly elusive Robocop as a sweetener before he eliminated Schultz.

Karim picked up the case with the money and started for the back door. At that moment, the sound of gunfire erupted outside. Dmitri twisted his head in the direction of the sounds. He saw the familiar face of the FBI agent Matt Higgins rushing toward the entrance. The face that Schultz had provided him with the first email appeared clearly in the store window.

"It's a trap. The FBI is here. Kill him." He pointed at the fleeing Karim as he shouted the order.

The gunman didn't hesitate a second. He swung the automatic weapon at the figure of Karim, who now ran at full steam to the exit.

The rifle erupted, spraying the man's back with multiple rounds. The body smashed against the door and collapsed.

"Get the case," he ordered as he saw the man talking into some device on his wrist.

Dmitri pulled his own pistol and moved toward the rear door. His man retrieved the case, handed it to him, and now turned to face the threat coming through the front door. He let loose a fusillade of rounds at the attacking FBI figure as the target barged through the door, but the bullets went wide of the moving agent and shattered the window behind him. The sound of shattering and collapsing glass filled the room intermingled with a deafening cacophony of sounds.

"Cover me," Dmitri said as he stood by his gunman who now prepared to fire again. The gun came up directly in front of his torso, pointing at his stomach.

"Duck," he heard the man command. As he fell to his knees, bullets whipped over his head. He crawled low toward the rear exit, and the weapon over his head unleashed another blistering discharge of multiple rounds.

Dmitri glanced backwards to see that the man had fired at the entrance and not at the location where the FBI agent remained behind a desk, where he had taken cover from the initial volley of automatic fire. Before he turned back, he observed a woman falling to the ground in front of the doorway.

"Get out. The car is coming around. I called for it," the man shouted into his ear. He swung his weapon to his target behind the desk and unleashed multiple rounds at the location where the FBI agent attempted to hide. That volley would keep him down for a few seconds, and those seconds were all they would need to escape the building.

Dmitri ran out the door with the case in his hand. As soon as he exited the building, his SUV came screeching to a halt a few feet away. Andreas pushed open the doors, and Dmitri and the man jumped in. The vehicle accelerated and peeled rubber for half a block.

* * *

MATT SAW THE WEAPON AND DOVE BEHIND A METAL DESK NEAR THE door into Karim's office. He started to rise up to return fire when he heard the door open again. Liz appeared with her weapon drawn. She fired two shots toward the man with the automatic weapon without taking time to aim. She must be trying to divert their attention away from him. She had certainly seen him dive for cover as the rounds came close to his head. Her intention became obvious to Matt —she wanted to force them to swing toward her to give Matt time to reach a firing position.

In what seemed like a microsecond, rounds from the automatic weapon plowed into Liz after she entered the door. Matt started to rise to return fire, but the shooter swiveled the rifle and more bullets impacted the desk where he hid. He dove back, crawled to a position a few feet from where he had been, and rose up to fire. There wasn't anything to shoot at. The back door slammed shut behind the last fleeing man. He vaulted up and ran to the rear door. On the way, he heard the screaming of tires of a vehicle and knew that he couldn't get them.

He rushed back to where Liz lay prone on the floor. He felt for a pulse. After a few seconds of agony as he prayed and attempted to locate one on her neck, he finally found one. On speed dial, he requested an ambulance and told the operator of the shooting that had taken place at his location. He checked Karim but found no pulse. The locals would have to be involved with a man shot out in the street, an FBI agent down with multiple gunshots, and the corpse of Karim.

He went to Liz and held her until the sound of the sirens reached him.

"You'll be okay. Just hang on," he whispered into her ear. He moved to rest her head in his lap. He rose only when the EMTs and the local police arrived. The medics took over and rushed Liz out on a gurney.

What a mess, flashed through Matt's mind.

46

TASHA CALLS

In the bathroom of the safe house in Alexandria, Tasha used the phone, which she kept in her purse. She wanted desperately to tell Papa she remained all right after the firefight at the house where they had detained her. She realized that her father must have sent one of the groups that had engaged in the firefight outside the house. He would be worried about her, since she had not been at the house.

"Papa," she said as soon as she heard his voice, "I wanted to tell you I'm safe. I saw the gunfight, but Matt Higgins rescued me from the kidnappers and got me away." She stopped and waited.

"Tasha, I'm so glad to hear from you. Where are you?"

"I'm in an apartment in Alexandria, Virginia. Scott and Gerti Donavan are giving me protection until you can come and get me. I wanna go home."

"Listen, Tasha, I can't come there. I want you to come to me. I'm in great danger here in the States. Some people are after me, trying to kill me, and I need to get on my plane to take us home. If you are safe, stay there and I can come back later to get you."

"No, wait. I'm sure I can sneak away from here. I can take a taxi to meet you. But the men who took me said you are a Russian gangster. Why would they say that, Papa?"

"No idea. I've always been a businessman, and a good one. One day you will take over the business I have built for you."

She heard someone approaching the bathroom.

"Where are you?"

"I'm on my way to the Manassas Regional Airport, to a hangar at the far end of the runway. There is no other building around us. Come as quickly as you can. We will be on the way home in a few hours. I can't be at the hangar for another hour, as I am obliged to make one stop on the way to reimburse a creditor. I'll wait on you."

He needed to clear his account with Artur and to thank him in person before he left. They'd changed cars a few minutes after the shooting at Karim's place as Dmitri believed the FBI would have all the police forces looking for that SUV.

"I'll be there. See you soon, Papa."

* * *

MILES AWAY, MATT LISTENED TO THE CONVERSATION. THIS COULD BE his last chance to get to Dmitri. The man would fly from America, and he would be back at square one. Now that he knew Dmitri's location, he could trap him, he thought.

He called Scott. "Scott, the girl is going to try to escape and run to her father. I just listened to their conversation. She's attempting to reach Manassas Regional Airport. You and Gerti need to contain her and bring her to that location."

"What do we do there?" Scott queried.

"We are going to get the truth out of that Russian. We might use his daughter to get him to talk since I don't have any other options at this time."

"We'll be on the way in a few minutes. I'll tell her we'll volunteer to take her to her father, if she knows where he is. I think she trusts us after we saved her from the kidnappers, and she might go along with us taking her there. I would also let Mr. Schultz know what we're doing. I'm sure Gerti wants to bring him up to date."

"Good luck, but one way or another, get her there."

* * *

Dmitri relaxed in the backseat of a white Cadillac as it sped toward the airfield. Things were going to work out. He would depart with his daughter. But another idea sprang into his head. This one he really liked, as it encompassed all the elements of a Greek drama.

His phone buzzed. The Robocop's voice boomed in his ear. "I received a call that informed me that Matt Higgins is going to the Manassas Regional Airport. Scott Donavan will also be there. No one else is to be harmed. Higgins knows that is where you are going. Fulfill your contract."

"You should come and see it fulfilled. You can then pay me for its completion."

The distorted voice said, "Agreed, I'm on my way."

47

LIZ AT THE HOSPITAL

MATT ACCOMPANIED LIZ ON THE AMBULANCE RIDE TO THE HOSPITAL. She remained conscious, but in a great deal of pain. The medics took her vitals and relayed them to a doctor at the hospital. With the sound of the wailing siren barely audible inside the speeding vehicle, he held her hand and told her she would make it when he saw her open her eyes. Liz seemed to go in and out of consciousness. On arrival at the hospital, the EMTs rushed her into a room, and Matt couldn't enter.

He waited for twenty minutes, and then a doctor came to him to report that Liz would make it, but would need to be hospitalized for a few days. She would require a period of physical therapy for her recovery. Matt thanked him and went outside to get a taxi to go back to Karim's to retrieve his car.

In the cab, he called Schultz.

"I need some help. I believe I've located Dmitri. Scott must have informed you of where we're going by now. I need some manpower. I lost my FBI support, but I could use some muscle. I know you have contacts, and when I take Dmitri down, I believe he'll have secured some local firepower. I can't call in the FBI because what I want to do is a little beyond their tolerance for unauthorized procedures, if you follow." Matt paused.

"I certainly do. Where and when do you need men?"

Matt told him.

"They will be there, and I will come with them. Give us thirty minutes."

Matt breathed a little easier. He estimated that Dmitri had lost some men here in the US, but they must have come from local contacts. If so, the man would again prevail upon his source to provide more guns to cover his departure. How many, Matt didn't know, but the last time there had been six or seven. He needed to get there as quick as possible to recon the area and prepare for Dmitri's arrival. If he could prevent the man from reaching the hangar with the aircraft, that would be the best solution. It would keep the plane out of play and eliminate that avenue of escape.

He called Scott. "Where are you?"

"Just a few minutes from the airfield."

"I should be there in three. Stay away from the hangar that he told Tasha to go to. We need to be wary. I don't think he's there yet, but I don't want us to walk up to it without knowing if he's there."

"What are you going to do?"

"I'm playing it by ear."

"No, I mean what are you going to do with Dmitri?"

"I want to find out why he came after us, or who put him up to it. He knows and I'll get it out of him." Matt hung up.

* * *

DMITRI HAD ARRIVED AT THE HANGAR WELL BEFORE MATT OR SCOTT. He was joined by the extra men provided by Artur. A few minutes later, he saw cars starting to arrive on the far end of the field. He knew this would be Higgins and his FBI friends. He remained confident that he could fulfill the contract and receive his money from Robocop, or the man he discovered behind the voice—Mr. Benjamin Schultz. He would then handle the last detail before his departure.

He and his daughter would fly to Russia, where they would be safe, and all on the list, plus Schultz, would be dead.

If he remained in the hangar with his men, Higgins and his group would have to approach. At that point, he would launch his attack when they were in the open and finish them off. The plan made sense to him, and he told the men around him what he intended to do.

"Wait until they approach. I want them to get close," he ordered.

They acknowledged his plan, and the five of them moved into position to gain the best fields of fire on anyone approaching.

Dmitri thanked his good fortune that he had arrived before them. Now he would destroy them. He held the upper hand.

48

MANASSAS REGIONAL AIRPORT

As Matt approached the airfield, he saw Schultz standing in front of the FBO. The Fixed Base Operations served as a gas station, eatery and general store for planes landing at the airport. As he looked around, however, he realized that this building couldn't be Dmitri's location. Matt pulled up beside the man and got out.

"Matt, I must apologize to you," Schultz said as soon as Matt approached. "I acted rashly in taking the girl. I wanted to get some leverage over Dmitri for his attempts to kill my daughter. I should have worked with you."

"I accept your apology, and, yes, it would've been much better if we'd coordinated our actions. I had no idea you were going to take any direct action on your own."

"You're correct. I will coordinate in the future," Schultz said.

Matt decided to let it go for the present as the man had plainly apologized and seemed eager to help at this stage of his operation.

"How many men do you have?" Matt asked.

"Four. Is that enough?"

"It'll do. I don't know how many men he has available, but we should be fine. I believe we're here before him. We can set up an ambush for his arrival. I want you to take half of your men and go to the rear of that hangar." Matt pointed at the distant hangar on the other side of the field, almost out of sight of the main buildings on the airfield. He had called the airport tower before his arrival and learned in which hangar Dmitri had positioned his plane.

"Can do. What are you going to do?"

"I'm working on it," Matt said with a smile. He realized that he needed to approach the building as fast as possible to secure it before Dmitri arrived. It would give them a tactical advantage to hold it.

"Scott told me he's bringing the girl here," Schultz said.

"Yes. I don't want her to get involved in any shoot-out. I'm actually hoping to avoid any weapons use in order to talk with him. Remember, the reason we're after Dmitri is to discover why he came after us, or who paid him to come after the three of us named in that email."

"True, so I'll take my men around to the rear, and once you secure the building, we'll come in and take up positions with you." He pointed at two of his men to stay with Matt and two to follow him. They climbed into an SUV and headed toward the hangar. Matt now had himself and two of Schultz's men. Scott and Gerti could augment his numbers when they arrived. He hoped all would go smoothly and they would finally uncover Dmitri's secret.

Matt decided to move and get into the building now. He signaled the two men to get into their SUV and he jumped into his car. Schultz's car disappeared behind the hangar, and Matt led the two-vehicle convoy toward the target.

* * *

Scott maintained a high rate of speed to reach the airfield. He wanted to arrive before anything happened. The phone call between Tasha and her father caused the girl to become quite somber. She must be confused with the happenings that now surrounded her father. She appeared to be struggling with some form of inner conflict, by the expression on her face and the fact the she had gone silent.

"Are you all right?" Gerti asked her.

"I don't understand. My father said he is only a businessman, but I get the feeling from the men who kidnapped me and to a lesser degree from you that he could be involved in some illegal activities. Is that right?"

"We're in no position to judge. We do know that he may be involved in an attempt on someone's life. That's why we want to talk to him and find out what he knows about it," Gerti said.

"I plan on asking him outright when we get there. He'll give me a truthful answer," Tasha said. "I have to know."

"We're at the airfield," Scott said. "I can see Matt's car, with another one moving toward the hangar your father told you about."

Matt's car stopped about a hundred feet from an entrance to the right of the large sliding door that allowed aircraft to enter and to exit. Scott headed directly for him and came to a screeching halt. Tasha immediately jumped out and started to run toward the hangar. Her action took Scott and Gerti by surprise.

"Stop," Gerti and Scott shouted together.

INSIDE THE HANGAR

DMITRI OBSERVED THE VEHICLES AS THEY HEADED TO THE REAR OF THE hangar. He pointed at three of his men and gestured for them to go to the back wall and cover that area. The men moved quickly, taking up positions covering the rear approach from the two four-panel windows on that wall. With those precautions in place, he again focused his attention outside to the front. A car and an SUV approached from that direction.

He surmised by their actions that his attackers had assumed that no one had entered the hangar. Otherwise, there would be no reason for someone to come streaming across an open airfield without first climbing out of their vehicles and slowly coming forward to see if anyone was there or if anyone fired at them. That would be the prudent move, not this blatant disregard for the safety of the men now approaching.

His thoughts were interrupted when another vehicle came flying across the tarmac and slid to a stop behind a car. He watched the FBI agent Higgins climb out of his car and head toward the car of the new arrival. Dmitri stood dumbfounded for a second. What the hell were they doing? Gathering reinforcements? His heart almost stopped as the car door swung open. He saw his daughter jump from the arriving vehicle and start to run toward the hangar. He had to rescue her, he told himself. The FBI couldn't capture her and use her against him.

"Hold your fire," he commanded.

What was going on? He decided to move. Then he saw Higgins rush to stop the girl and pull her back to where his group stood near the car.

This caused Dmitri's blood pressure to spike. He could hear his heart pumping in his chest. He must rescue his daughter, and get her away from the FBI. His mind only saw his darling girl in peril. He needed to get her and take her back to Russia.

"Get ready. We're going out there and saving my daughter. Watch where you shoot. Don't hit her. We need to secure her. Bring her in here and you two open the hangar doors. The pilots have already pre-flighted the plane and are in the cockpit ready to go."

He looked at each man. "Ready?"

Each gave him a nod of understanding. Maybe this wasn't his brightest move, attacking a group while in the open, but he had to get his little girl away from them.

"Open the door," he commanded.

* * *

"What is she trying to do?" Matt asked Scott.

"I think she's really confused about her father. All her life, he's been a businessman to her. Now she's wondering what he really is and wants to confront him," Gerti added.

"She's really wound tight," Scott added.

Matt watched Tasha for a few seconds before he spoke to her. "I know this may be very difficult for you, but there's a possibility of real danger here. I don't want you hurt. We're going to try and take your father into custody to ask him some questions. It could be nothing, but we need to find some things out. Please control yourself until we sort this out with your father. You will be able to talk to him when we do. I promise. So I'm asking you to calm down."

He observed the young lady for a few seconds and saw her relax her shoulders, which he took as a subtle telltale capitulation in her manner. Then, looking him in the eye, she slowly nodded her head in silent agreement.

"Gerti, you stay here with Tasha while we go and check out the hangar. Your father is around back setting up a blocking position there in case we need it," Matt said. He turned to Schultz's men. "All right, let's go check out the hangar."

The sound of gunfire erupted at that moment. Bullets whizzed by, barely missing his head.

50

THE ASSAULT

DMITRI LED THE CHARGE OF HIS MEN AS THEY RAN TO WHERE HE observed Tasha being held by the FBI agent. He fired his handgun, a 9mm Glock, at the extra security men he saw who stood away from his daughter. He didn't want to hit her with stray rounds. He nailed one of the men, who reached for his weapon. The man fell. The men beside him fired as they ran over the one hundred feet that separated the cars from the front of the hangar. One of the men next to him fell as return fire sliced into the Russian assault.

Dmitri saw the men near the cars try to get behind them. Everyone seemed to be firing at once. As he neared the FBI agent Higgins, he pointed his weapon at the man and fired. Higgins released the grip he had on Tasha arm and spun, falling backwards to the ground.

Dmitri rushed to his daughter. He hugged her, took her hand, and then led her back toward the safety of the hangar. She offered some light resistance to his efforts to get her to follow, but he used his superior force to propel her forward for only a few more feet. He eventually got behind her and pushed her toward the door.

She screamed as a bullet whizzed past her head. The next

moment, she felt her father's grip release her arm as he stumbled forward.

* * *

MATT CLEARLY SAW DMITRI AS THE MAN CHARGED OUT OF THE HANGAR. It took him a second to realize he held a raised weapon and, almost simultaneously, he heard the gun discharge. It looked like the five assailants were planning to overrun them by sheer force. Matt pulled his weapon and tried to move Tasha to a position behind the car. She seemed frozen in place, and he couldn't get her to move with his gentle pulling. He reached up to get a better grip on her arm in order to force her to accompany him to the safety of the vehicles.

As he turned to yell to the others to get behind the cars, he felt the searing hot pain of a bullet ripping through his shoulder. He recognized the hurt from a previous experience with getting shot. It felt like he had been hit with a baseball bat swung by a professional player. The impact of the round compelled him to release his grip on Tasha. He also began to spin around and then realized he was falling to the ground.

Landing on his back, he felt his head ricochet off the tarmac of the taxiway, producing instant and intense pain in his head. His vision now showed two or three images of people instead of one. He thought for a few seconds that he would lose it, then willed himself to regain control and swung himself into a sitting position. He must get back in the fight.

Weapons were firing all around him. His vision began to clear, and he concentrated on following the girl being dragged by Dmitri. He pushed the pain and the shock from his mind. He needed to have his wits about him or he would surely be killed. Seeing his pistol a foot from his right leg, he grabbed for it and pulled it up to a firing position. At the entrance to the hangar, he watched as Dmitri moved behind his daughter and attempted to push her inside.

The remaining men of the assault force tried to cover his retreat into the hangar. The heavy volume of fire from the men around Matt had a devastating effect on their efforts, and they began to fall before Dmitri reached his destination.

Dmitri, delayed by his daughter's reluctance, struggled to push her forward. This provided Matt with a singular opportunity he could not pass up.

With clear vision, and using both hands, he kept his eyes open. His entire focus centered on the back of the man who now loomed in his gun's sight. His left shoulder shot agony that reached his brain. He involuntarily flinched. The sight on his weapon fell off the spot he aimed at. From some depth in his mind, he disregarded his pain and regained clarity. With his blurry vision, he reacquired Dmitri with his weapon. As the Russian rushed to the door, Matt squeezed the trigger as gently as he could in order not to be off target.

He saw the round enter the back of Dmitri Alexandrovitch. The man lunged forward, trying to push his daughter and himself to safety. Around Matt, weapons fire raged as the others of Dmitri's assault team fell one by one in their attempts to get back inside the hangar.

"Cease fire," Matt ordered. The ringing in his ears caused by the explosion of the fired rounds lingered for a few seconds.

At last, silence settled on the field.

51

CONFRONTATION WITH DMITRI

Matt regained his footing, as he disregarded the excruciating pain from his wound, and then ran toward the fallen figure in the hangar doorway. He reached Dmitri, where his daughter caressed his body and cradled his head in her arms when she collapsed to a sitting position. He heard Dmitri say, "That's enough. No more fighting." The men inside the hangar lowered their weapons as Matt knelt beside the prone man.

"You bastard, you killed Bridget. I'm glad I shot you."

"You don't know, do you?" Dmitri struggled with his words.

"What do you mean? Who initiated the contract to kill Bridget, Scott and me?"

Dmitri coughed. A little blood appeared on his lips.

"Leave him alone," shouted Tasha, but her father waved her concern away.

"There is only one person who could have made all these things happen to you over the last few weeks," Dmitri said, his voice growing quieter. "There is only one individual who had the best opportunity to clone your phone, and only one who promised to release the sniper if he told you the order came from the Vatican. He bribed the man to tell you that lie when he gave the signal, which was to give him a cup of water." Dmitri took a deep breath. He seemed to enjoy the transformation he witnessed on Matt's face as he continued.

"I had the torturers tortured to find that out. Who could have warned me before you arrived in Russia, so that I got away and planned an attack on you? Who knew you were coming to Russia?"

"Please, leave him alone," Tasha begged. "You can see he is dying."

Dmitri slumped lower in his daughter's arms. He looked up at Matt with eyes that began to lose focus. "You know who that is. I only ask that you take care of Schultz for me. He is the one who paid for the contract."

Matt heard the man breathe his last. Tasha wailed a mournful cry. No other sound filled the air.

* * *

GERTI AND SCOTT ARRIVED AT THE BUILDING'S DOOR SECONDS AFTER Matt reached Dmitri. They had checked the downed men out front on the tarmac and had taken their weapons before proceeding to the entrance. Gerti arrived first and stooped down behind Matt to hear what the man said.

Gerti and Scott both heard Dmitri's revelation.

Gerti jumped up as the man expired. She shouted, "No way. He's lying."

Scott grabbed her and tried to hold her. She broke free and jerked Matt up from his kneeling position by the collar. He turned to face her, and in a momentary glance to his left, he observed Schultz returning from the rear of the building, where he had been a blocking force to prevent anyone from escaping through that exit. He approached enough to hear his daughter's outburst.

"That's a goddamn lie. My father didn't do that," she shouted at Matt. Gerti wanted to convey her indignation at the accusations made by Dmitri against her father. They couldn't be true. He would never try to kill her husband. Her father had arranged for their marriage. It didn't make any sense. Why Bridget and Matt? She felt her whole world crumbling. Her father could settle all this. Where could he be?

In her mind, the facts the dead man had revealed cut through her veil of absolute deniability. In reality, she could not come to grips with the idea that the man would lie as he died. For what purpose? The answer was obvious—there existed no reason. How could this be happening to her? Her whole world now collapsed around her.

"No, it's not true," But each word came out softer, and tears filled her face. "It's not true."

Gerti saw Matt pull his weapon when Schultz approached.

52

CONFESSION

Schultz had heard the ferocious gun battle that erupted on the other side of the hangar from where he guarded the rear entrance. He waited, but nothing appeared at the rear of the hangar. So he decided to move to reinforce the men in the front, and to be able to carry out his own new plan.

Dmitri hadn't fulfilled his contract. The time had arrived for Schultz to take matters into his own hands. He needed to act while mayhem abounded. The firefight provided that cover. He would kill the objects of his hatred himself. If his luck held, he could also eliminate Dmitri. The moment for him to exact his secret vendetta on Matt and Scott had arrived.

He believed his daughter would understand once he showed her that he had done all this for her. Gerti shared the same genes as he did and had developed a similar sense of duty to that which he professed. The family came first, and any action taken to secure that would be justified in the long run. He often saw her act with the same ruthlessness as himself when she needed to, and he counted on that now. She must see that he had to do this for the good of the family, and out of his need to punish his targets for what they had done.

While he went around the hangar, he quickly reviewed the

compelling reasons for why he had finally targeted them for elimination. He'd learned that Bridget had purposely left his son die on the battlefield because she'd treated another soldier first. After Bridget had left the Army, he'd lost her for some time, but a friend from his college days had told him about the archaeological dig their university had sponsored and that Bridget held a place on the team. He'd used contract killers to eliminate her on the archaeology site, but the men had failed. After thinking both assassins dead for months, he'd received a call from one man and had again sent him to get the Donavan girl. He'd botched it and lost his life.

Matt Higgins had to go because of his association with the Donavans. If he were left alive, he would eventually work everything out and come after him for Bridget's sake. While Schultz had requested Matt to interrogate the man who'd shot at his daughter and almost killed her, he'd told the shooter that, when he gave him a cup of water, he was to tell Higgins that the email came from the Vatican. If the man would do this, he would release him afterwards. The deception would allow Dmitri to get his targets into a known position where he could act. He'd provided the hit man in Rome with the details of their trip. The man had failed to kill Scott and Matt while they searched for the source of the emails.

Bridget and Scott had once saved him after a crazed newspaperman had tried to blackmail him. That wasn't enough to make him forgive her, though, because he also held them accountable for ripping him off for five million dollars. During that same period, while hunting for the Bible of Constantine, Scott had participated in an event in which his daughter had received a severe knife wound that could have killed her. He couldn't forgive Scott for that. Next time around him, she could not be so lucky as to survive.

He'd felt sure his problems would be eliminated when he gave Dmitri their schedule for going to Russia, and yet again he'd experienced failure. The romance with Scott presented a potential disaster for his girl, but he knew she would get over him, especially if she produced a baby. That would take her mind off the loss of her husband.

On arriving at the front of the hangar, he felt joy in seeing Dmitri lying on the ground, apparently dead. His daughter's reaction to the events immediately preceding his arrival caused him to stop. The bastard must have confessed in his dying breath. Gerti had heard about everything from the Russian instead of the way he'd wanted to present it to her.

He moved forward to where Dmitri lay and reached to draw his weapon. His breath came in short gulps, and his hand started to tremble when it reached for his gun. Before he grabbed it, and before he could take another step, Matt jumped up and jammed his weapon up under his chin so quickly that he couldn't move or counter the attack.

Schultz cried out, "What are you doing? I came around to support you."

53

MATT CONFRONTS SCHULTZ

M ATT'S MIND SWIRLED AS HE PUSHED THE GUN UP UNDER SCHULTZ'S chin. He tried to confront the disbelief, the confusion, and the shock he felt from the revelations made by Dmitri. The events enumerated by the Russian now made perfect sense and exactly fit the experiences of the last weeks. The man knew all the facts and the dealings that had shaped his pursuit of the man behind Bridget's murder.

There appeared to be only one inevitable conclusion. Deep within himself, he realized the man had spoken the truth. Now the man who had ordered the love of his life murdered stood directly in front of him, his hands in clear view. No weapon was in sight, and he did not appear to pose an imminent threat. Matt relaxed his position and slowly lowered his gun hand from the man's face. He had sworn to kill the bastard who'd contracted their deaths, but cold-blooded murder didn't reside in his being.

"How could you do this? You arranged to have Bridget killed and planned to murder Scott and me. You are going to jail for a long time." Matt moved to put handcuffs on him. No instant justice to be administered here, especially not from the barrel of his weapon.

Then with speed he did not believe Schultz possessed, the man's hands became a blur. With one hand he shoved Matt backwards, and the other pulled a Glock. He started firing as the gun came out. The pistol not aimed yet at any specific target, bullets flew around the hangar. Matt recovered, but he saw Schultz continue to pull the trigger as he swung it directly at him. Bullets continued to spew from the weapon as Schultz maintained a steady volume of fire.

With both eyes open, Matt, with absolute confidence in his ability to stop this, raised his weapon to a firing position. Schultz appeared in his sight, and without pausing, he fired. Then, he pulled the trigger again and saw the bullets enter Schultz in the center of his torso.

A glass-shattering scream filled the hangar.

* * *

GERTI COULDN'T CONTROL HERSELF. SHE EMITTED THE SOUL-PIERCING scream as she saw her father's body tumble forward after Matt's shots. The reverberation of the pistol's explosive firing still lingered. She couldn't comprehend that her father had been shot dead. She raced at Matt and started to pummel him with her fists while continuing the unrelenting screaming and profanity directed at him.

"You bastard," were the kindest words to emanate from her mouth. The fury spewing from her knew no bounds. Her father was dead, and Matt had killed him.

"You didn't have to murder him," she shouted.

She drew in a long deep breath. Her hatred of this man would never end. She would see to it that he paid for this. In her mind, she felt the presence of her father. He would have said the same thing and thought the same thoughts. After all these years, he had been right. She embodied a mirror image of him, no matter what she tried to change.

Someone shouted her name. She didn't want to turn away from the object of her hate.

"Gerti." Then louder: "Gerti!"

She let her name enter her awareness, by the force of the voice calling. Who yelled her name? It sounded like it came up from the ground.

"What?" she screamed. She looked down to the figure of Tasha, still clutching her dead father's head. The girl's face resembled a fountain of tears. She had been crying uncontrollably since her father had died in her arms. She pointed, with her raised hand, to behind Gerti.

"Look," she commanded.

With a great effort, Gerti looked in the direction that the girl indicated. She couldn't believe it. Her mind unable to comprehend what she saw.

"Oh my God, no. *No!*"

She rushed over to where Scott lay on the floor. Blood poured from his mouth, and his eyes were growing dim. She crouched to a position beside him. She quickly sat on the floor and took his head in her hands.

"Don't leave me. I love you." She tried to say each word clearly so he would comprehend.

He moved his lips. She bent down close to his mouth to hear.

"I love you," came out in a prolonged utterance, and then his eyes glazed over and his head dropped.

Gerti hugged him in a longing embrace. Her whole body trembled, and her mind felt shattered at the loss of her father and now her husband in a matter of minutes. To her, Scott's death had resulted because Matt had shot at her father and that had caused him to spray rounds all over. Two of the bullets had stricken her husband, the father of her unborn child.

She gritted her teeth so hard her whole jaw felt like exploding. This reaction provided her a modicum of clarity. She didn't want to take the time to think of the future in her present state of mind. There would be time for that, and for the actions she knew in her soul that she would be capable of. Father's instructions on how to do business were no longer lost on her. She knew what she had to do, and without remorse, she consciously acknowledged that she embodied the essence of her father at her very core.

Now the time for grief and sorrow had arrived. She must deal with that and get through to the other side before doing anything else. She fell over her husband's body and let her tears flow.

54

FUNERAL

Matt stood bareheaded in the rain by the gravesite. The burial ceremony for Scott Donavan had finished a few minutes before. People were still milling around and saying their goodbyes. Matt looked at the casket, and his mind went to all the adventures he shared with this man. Scott had exhibited great courage in Tel Aviv in the rescue of Bridget from the rapist.

He stood steadfast in supporting his sister's efforts to acquire the Bible of Constantine. In Matt's effort to bring a jihadist down in Savannah to stop an arms-importing ring, Scott had played an instrumental role in achieving the destruction of that cell. Scott had also helped him solve the mystery of who'd ordered Bridget's murder.

Scott Donavan was a brave man, and one Matt would sorely miss. He looked around and saw Gerti approaching him. She had not spoken to him once since they'd departed that hangar, not even at her father's funeral. He profoundly regretted what had happened, but he realized that his actions had been completely justified.

"Gerti, please accept my condolences," Matt said as she neared.

"I'm going to New York. We will never have any future personal connections. Do not call me." She turned her hate-filled eyes away and walked off.

Matt stood shocked. They had been through so much, and now she treated him like a dog who had pooped on the living room rug. He tried to understand her position, but his logic told him that his actions in the hangar were completely warranted. He'd only wanted to save lives by stopping the man from firing a weapon at people. Unfortunately, it hadn't worked out that way. She now seemed to blame him for all that had happened. He acknowledged that some responsibility fell on his shoulders, but not all of it, as she'd intimated.

He walked away and headed over to Bridget Donavan's grave. He didn't watch the time, so he had no idea of how long he stood there going over their lives together, from the early days in the Army up to her brutal murder, engineered by Schultz. The loss of his love still pained him deeply. He decided that he needed a drink. From this day forward, things were going to change in his life.

The next morning, Matt visited Liz in the hospital. She still experienced pain when she moved.

"It's getting better. At least it doesn't hurt every time I breathe." She smiled as she said this. She still looked pale and weak. Matt enjoyed the short visit. He felt extremely glad that Liz would fully recover. She would be back on her feet in a few weeks.

The FBI director arrived to visit his special assistant. Matt said his farewells and departed.

"How are you?" asked the director.

"Getting better every day. I'll be back to work in a few days."

"Did you tell him yet?"

"No," she said.

"When?"

"It's not time yet. In a few weeks, after he processes the events that just transpired. He'll take it pretty hard, and I want to make sure I do it at the best time."

"Okay. I'll leave it to you to arrange everything."

* * *

MATT LEFT THE HOSPITAL, AND THE NEXT DAY, WITH SET determination, he drove to the FBI building. Over the last few days, he had run this whole FBI thing around in his head and concluded that all their rules were too restrictive. If they wanted him to do certain jobs, there were always too many rules, too much oversight. The Bureau usually tried to put strings on all his activity. Earlier that morning, he'd phoned the director and asked if he could stop by. The director had given him a time, and Matt arrived a few minutes early. He took a seat in the outer office and waited.

The silver-haired man with the familiar face of the director appeared at the appointment time. He gave Matt a firm handshake and an accompanying smile.

"Come on in," he said as he led Matt into his office.

The place seemed bigger than Matt remembered. Then again, on earlier occasions, he'd generally entered this place to argue or plead for something. He hadn't taken notice of the pictures of the director and the president, the university diplomas and the large picture of J. Edgar Hoover.

"Matt, you have done everything I asked of you, and in a superb fashion. After the gun battle at the airport and Agent Garcia's wounds, I think you must take some time off."

"I appreciate that, sir. I have another plan." He took out his credentials and his weapon and placed them on the director's desk. "I need a vacation from the FBI. It's time for me to go my own way. I lost too much lately, and I plan to start over."

"I'm sorry to see you go. You know we still need men like you. I now have to find someone to fill the SOE billet that you have filled so admirably."

"It's time for someone else to fill it. Good-bye, sir."

* * *

GERTI TOOK TASHA ON THE COMPANY JET TO NEW YORK. THE TWO girls had bonded quickly and at a basic level, with both suffering from the loss of their respective fathers. During the lawyer's presentation the next day, Gerti learned what her new empire consisted of. The sums were well beyond anything she had ever imagined.

She inquired of Tasha if she wanted her to accompany her to Russia to hear the reading of her father's will and what she now would acquire. Five days later, they heard the Russian lawyer reveal the numbers and possessions that Tasha had inherited from her father. She revealed to Gerti that she couldn't believe all that she would inherit.

That night, before going to sleep, Gerti realized that she now controlled a multibillion-dollar organization. In order for it to succeed, she would have to take hold of the reins and run it like her father had. She knew she could. She remained her father's daughter and currently exhibited all of his traits. Perhaps she had inherited the characteristics she'd despised in her father until recently.

She realized that trying to turn into a stay-at-home mother behind a white fence that she and Scott dreamed of would not now be possible. The unreachable dream Matt Higgins had destroyed. She now needed to forge ahead in a different direction for herself and for her unborn child.

"Gerti, do you think you might want to work together? We could do some great business things by uniting on some aspects of our operation," Tasha suggested over a glass of vodka.

"My thoughts exactly." Gerti smiled and they clinked glasses.

In the recesses of her mind, the idea of vengeance emerged, the same way she had visualized it would in her father. With the assets she now commanded, and the reach of her new, combined organizations, she decided to take all the steps required.

With venom in her voice, she said aloud, "Matt Higgins, you are as good as dead."

EPILOGUE

Lying on a beach near Buckroe Beach, Virginia, Matt rolled over to get some tan on his back. The morning sun emerged into a midday scorcher. He wanted to rub some cream on his back but knew he couldn't reach all the spots. Next visit to the seashore, he'd buy some of that spray-on sunscreen that he could use to cover his back.

The real reason he probably couldn't reach his back belonged to the throbbing hangover he experienced from the huge amount of vodka consumed the evening before. In addition, he did not consider the still-healing gunshot wound received from Dmitri. At night, his mind drifted to Bridget; then he would bring out the booze in his hotel room. This happened too often, and he knew it.

A gust of wind pushed sand into his mouth. He tried to spit it out, but some remained. He desired to get a drink, a hair-of-the-dog type drink that might mitigate the effects of the hangover and stop the throbbing.

Two weeks after he'd quit the FBI, his father had passed. The old man had left him over twenty million dollars in his hedge fund account. He couldn't process that big a number, so he'd decided to return to the place of his birth and lay by the sea to see what he wanted to do. After a week, he hadn't gotten very far and felt as lost as the day he'd arrived.

This afternoon, he planned to go and look at some places to buy. He wanted to decorate a place to be his own—not a house in the suburbs, but something that would be unique to him. He had no idea what that might be, but he would start to look for it soon.

Today, however, he would remain here, drink beer, and think about Bridget. That sounded like a good plan. He reminded himself that he had no Bridget, no future, no plans worth a damn, and no job.

While he cogitated on all his predicaments, he committed the error of not paying attention to his surroundings. Not like a former special operator in the military nor a trained FBI agent to commit such a breach. He failed to keep his situational awareness sharp and operating.

Without any warning, a lady stealthily came up and lay down near him. He hadn't noticed her approach. The first thing he heard was the sound of a woman's voice next to him. It startled him. He turned and saw a beautiful blond-headed woman of about his same age. She rose up on one arm with her palm under her head as she lay on her side.

"I've been looking for you, Mr. Matt Higgins. I hope I've allowed enough time for your grief, but now we need you." Her voice sounded familiar.

"Who's we?"

She rolled over and stood up. With a look over her shoulder, she said, "Come, follow me, and see."

THE END

FREE NOVELLA: To receive your free copy of the exclusive Donavan Adventure series novella *Secret of the Assassin* (not available anywhere else), visit **tomhaase.com/assassin.**

BETRAYED ANGEL (EXCERPT)

Former soldier Chuck McGregor is done with combat and itching for something to do. He's got wealth on his side, but no direction to guide him. For now, he spends his days on the Georgia beach and his nights drinking too much. He has no job, no friends, no purpose.

Until one day on the beach he hears a young woman scream, fighting to get away from two men. When he goes to help, one of them pulls a gun. And, as the men drag the girl away, Chuck McGregor finds his new purpose: save this girl he's never met. No matter the cost.

1
___

Chuck McGregor heard the scream. He raised his head off the sun-drenched sand, lifted his Georgia Bulldog baseball cap up, adjusted his sunglasses, and then looked around. He could see no one as the sound faded away without recurring. He reclined back into the warm sand.

He then rolled over to get some tan on his back, still expecting he might hear the sound again, but no scream came. In the war-torn cities of his recent past experiences, he would have reacted differently to any scream, but here in the safety of the American homeland, not so much.

Without success, he attempted to cover all of his back with sunblock. On his next visit to the beach, he'd have to buy some of that spray sunscreen that he could use to reach those areas. A cool ocean breeze provided light relief from the intensity of the scorching noonday heat. A soothing warmth radiated from the sand on this section on the nearly deserted beach at Tybee Island, near Savannah, Georgia.

Then the scream came again. At least it sounded like a scream. But the wind and the roaring of the waves as they rolled in made him decide it must be some kids screaming as they played a game. It sounded far away, and again the sound didn't repeat. Not hearing more, he scrunched his shoulders deeper into the warmth of the sand as his mind contemplated the immediate problems facing his life. He hoped the kids he had seen when he'd arrived had moved away or left the area and would stop screaming.

He returned his focus to the problem of his back but realized the primary reason he couldn't reach that area was probably the uncoordinated effort he exerted due to the substantial amount of vodka consumed the evening before. Every night, his mind drifted to what a miserable life he now led, and then he would bring out the booze in his hotel room. This scenario happened too often, and he recognized it for what it was—an escape mechanism.

A sudden gust of wind pushed some sand into his mouth. He tried to spit it out, but some grit remained. He needed to get a drink, the hair-of-the-dog type drink. That might take the edge off and stop the beginnings of an incipient throbbing headache. For days he had sat in his room and consumed only Raisin Bran cereal, alcohol, and little else. A habit began to emerge where he stared at a blank TV in his room for hours, contemplating his situation but not producing any focus for his life. His life, he laughed, as the life he knew, had ended when he'd left the Army.

Ten days after he'd recently separated from the Army, his father had passed.

"Why did you go into the Army? You'll never get rich there and you'll be wasting your life." His father used to say. The old man had never forgiven him for joining the service and had done everything to get him to leave.

"Come and join me as my partner. We have a multimillion-dollar business. You can have a safe and secure life." The old man had repeated this at every opportunity.

Now it was too late. His old man had left him over twenty million dollars in his inherited hedge fund account which was in his and his father's name, thereby bypassing the probate that might have been required. He had access to it immediately, but couldn't readily get his head around that big of a number.

His mind raced over his life. After college, Chuck had spent two years on the Savannah police force before deciding to join the Army after a painful divorce. He had loved the military, but he knew his sell-by date had arrived after all the tours to jihadist territories on special missions and the loss of friends there. He had lost his drive, and with reluctance, he knew it was time to get out. So, he'd decided to return to the place of his birth after his father's funeral and lay by the sea to ponder what he might do. After a week, the process hadn't gotten very far, and he felt just as lost and down on himself as the day he'd arrived in Georgia.

Today, he planned to go and look at some places to buy. He wanted to get a place to fix up to be his own, not a house in the suburbs, but something that would be unique to him. He entertained no ideas on what that might be, but he would start to look for it today.

Then again, maybe he would just stay here today and drink beer and think about things and what would he do with his life. That sounded like a better plan. He reminded himself that he had no one to love, no future, no plans worth a damn, and no job. On the other hand, he was rich.

While he cogitated on all his predicaments as he lay there, he committed the error of not paying attention to his surroundings. It was not like a former special operator for the Defense Intelligence Agency, the DIA, in the military to commit such a breach. He failed to keep his situational awareness sharp.

He vaguely heard the sound of a nearby muffled scream. Then the sound of sand being kicked reached his ears. He instinctively rotated his head toward the intrusive noise that now drew nearer. Probably those bothersome kids who had been playing on the beach had returned.

His sunglasses hid the direction his eyes looked. When he raised the bill of his cap, he observed two men who appeared to be pulling a woman along. They were closing to within ten feet of where he lay. He could see from the way she resisted that their actions militated against her free will. She let out another muffled scream that was stifled by the man's hand over her mouth. In a sudden flash, he wondered if she had made the earlier screams before the men had grabbed her.

"Move, you bitch," he heard one man say.

Squinting his eyes, he could see one man was white and one black. The woman, barely more than a girl, possessed the dark complexion of what he assumed to be some Hispanic lineage. Even through the sunglasses, he observed her beauty and calculated her age at late teens or early twenties at most.

"Let me go. You don't own me," came from the woman when the man removed his hand after she bit him.

"Yes, we do. You ran away. You're our property. You need to understand that. We bought and paid for you." The blond man put his hand back over her mouth.

They pulled her forward in a direction that took them directly beside Chuck. He could see that the two men possessed powerful physiques, evoking the image of bodyguards or barroom bouncers.

His sense of honor and his moral compass said he needed to act to help the young lady. He moved his hands, intending to raise himself up. He would see what this was about, but before he could move, the black one, seeing him making an effort to get up, pulled up his shirt, exposing a gun under his loose-fitting garment.

"Stay still, buddy. This is none of your business."

Chuck's earlier failure to keep his guard up now precluded him from acting. They were probably both armed, and he had no weapons. He knew better than to engage in a fistfight against a gun— a no-win situation for him. He relaxed back to his supine position and memorized the faces of the thugs. The image of the girl was already imprinted in his mind.

What did they mean by their comment that they had bought and paid for her? Was this some form of slavery? Perhaps she had run off after they'd paid her for sex—would that account for the "paid for" comment?

The three figures progressed rapidly up to the road behind the beach and disappeared while Chuck was still processing the scene he'd just witnessed. In his world, this type of treatment couldn't be condoned.

As a person searching for something to do, perhaps he'd look into this. He would find out what had happened to this young lady. On a scale of one to ten, doing something beat the hell out of lying on the beach all day. His whole adult life had been one of action, not lounging around, feeling sorry for himself like he'd been doing lately. He needed to get a grip and get moving, become engaged again in this new non-military world.

He got up, collected his things, and left the beach, heading for his hotel in downtown Savannah in a rental car. While driving, he came to the conclusion that he needed to tell the cops about the events on the beach. He hated bullies like the two goons who'd dragged the young girl off the beach. His sense of right and wrong rose up and slapped him in the face. The girl, he was certain, hadn't given her consent to the event.

He dialed 911 on his cell and told the operator what he'd witnessed.

When he reached downtown, he parked the car into a public parking garage, walked out onto Liberty Street and strolled toward his hotel.

On the side of the street at the corner of Liberty and Bull, he saw a cop car. It took him back to years ago when he had served on the Savannah police force. They were decent years, except for that one ass, his sergeant. The force had in fact prepared him in some ways for his military service. He waited for the signal to change and the white walk man signal to appear. He approached the cruiser.

He believed the girl on the beach had been in trouble, especially when he'd perceived her pleading eyes filled with tears. What did it mean that the men had claimed the girl belonged to them? Perhaps slavery? Or perhaps sex gone bad, and she had run off. One thing for sure, the girl had been terrified.

The police officer looked up as Chuck drew next to the cruiser.

Chuck saw an officer sitting in the car with his face in the shadow of a live oak tree. The tree's branches possessed an abundance of hanging Spanish moss. The cop's head rotated down to read something, but he looked up when he noticed Chuck's approach.

The officer, whose face remained in the shadow, looked at Chuck for a few seconds.

"Chuck," the cop eventually said.

Chuck was taken aback at hearing his name. How could the officer possibly know him?

"With the hat covering most of your face and the few days' stubble, I didn't recognize you. You look a lot older." The cop turned more toward him and moved out of the shadows. Chuck could now see his face.

"Eddie?" Chuck spoke in amazement. At that moment, he recognized his old partner, Eddie Gordon.

"I thought you were in the Army," Eddie said.

"Was till recently."

"Why are you back here?"

"Had to go somewhere, so I came back to my roots," Chuck said. "Did you get the info I called in on the girl taken on Tybee?"

"Heard it on the radio. What you saw is undoubtedly human traffickers at work on Tybee. We don't have the manpower to do much about it, even though we try. It's a crime hardly anyone reports, especially the girls."

"I want to find out more about it," Chuck said.

"Those guys play rough. If you get mixed up with them, you better be prepared for some bad shit."

"They won't know what hit them when a combat-trained soldier engages them," Chuck said with a grin.

"Well, if you want to know more about that business, I know a place where you might start. A local bar named Bronco on Habersham. The bartender might know something. I know him and he is pretty straight if he likes you."

"Thanks, Eddie. Let's get together and have a few." Chuck looked around and saw another cop car approaching.

"Sounds good. Here's my number." He handed Chuck a business card with the police logo and his number.

"See you soon," Chuck said and walked away, heading to his hotel.

Chuck thought that on his scale of one to ten, doing something moved the number up the ladder to at least a five in his rock bottom condition, while still unsuccessfully trying to figure out what to do with the rest of his life.

From deep within himself, his Army Airborne training told him it was time to get going. He set himself a new mission, just like in the Army. Find out about the damsel in distress and maybe ride to her rescue. He smiled to himself at that image. Perhaps a modern Don Quixote? No, he couldn't see that happening, but he laughed for the first time in weeks. As he walked along, he thought that perhaps he had found a new path forward.

END OF EXCERPT

Don't miss **BETRAYED ANGEL**, now available on Amazon in eBook and paperback!

ABOUT THE AUTHOR

TOM HAASE is the author of the Donavan Adventure series and Chuck McGregor Coastal Adventure series.

Tom had a thrilling experience when he jumped out of an airplane for the first time as an Army paratrooper in the 82nd Airborne Division. During his distinguished 28 year military career, Tom lived in Korea, Nepal, Ireland, Greece, England, and Cyprus. He had the honor of commanding a firing battery in combat in Viet Nam and representing the Department of Defense as a United States diplomat and Defense Attaché in four embassies. After retiring from the U.S. Army as a Lieutenant Colonel, he flew as a commercial pilot for a regional airline, and was rated to fly the Boeing 737.

Now, instead of flying airplanes or jumping out of them, he writes complex, fast-paced adventure novels to thrill readers.

He lives in Savannah, Georgia with his wife, Kate.

To learn more about his latest books, please visit tomhaase.com.

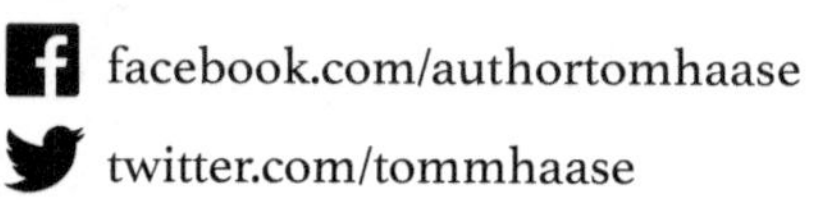